Praise for
Daniel Fights a Hurricane

"Shane Jones's *Daniel Fights a Hurricane* is a hypercolor kind of dream machine. Images of McMuffins morph to underwater cities morph to dream salesmen to brutal weather that can destroy the world itself. In midst of such imagination is an even richer field of complex emotion, collaged from the more abstract and terrifying ways that line our days. Here is a work that invents its own fundamental image, logic, and function, and somehow makes it feel like our new electric human skin."

—Blake Butler, author of *Scorch Atlas* and *Nothing*

"A quietly deft and linguistically playful book about the struggle between so-called reality and the realities of the imagination. *Daniel Fights a Hurricane* is about the way realities cross, collide, and twine around each other, and the lives that are wounded by being caught in between."

—Brian Evenson, author of *Fugue State*

Praise for
Light Boxes

"Resplendent, and somehow nearly edible, Shane Jones has written the kind of novel that makes you reconsider the word *perfect*." —Rivka Galchen, author of *Atmospheric Disturbances*

"An enchanting and witty fable . . . There are marvelous sentences throughout . . . Jones handles imagery like a gifted poet." —*Bookforum*

"We were completely blown away by Shane Jones's 2010 debut novel *Light Boxes*, a surreal, fabulistic tale of a village revolting against its never-ending February." —*Flavorpill*

"A literary gem of metaphysical malaise." —*Booklist*

"Magical . . . Jones's spare, alliterative sentences are flawless and sometimes delightful."   —*Time Out New York*

"At last, a book that cries out to our inner balloonists. Shane Jones has built a fable that is fresh and surprising, but also familiar in the way that the oldest stories are familiar. I recommend keeping a copy or two handy at all times."
                    —Jedediah Berry, author of *The Manual of Detection*

"Shot through with lyrical brilliance."   —*The Austin Chronicle*

"A slim and absorbing novel . . . kept afloat by a sea of imagery, both haunting and strange."   —*BlackBook*

"Jones has written a tale that is dreamy yet personal, experimental yet accessible."   —Michael Johnson, *Publishers Weekly*

"Reading this book makes you realize what our American literature has been missing. Wholly original, tremendously imaginative, written with the deftest hand, *Light Boxes* makes sense of modern life in the way that only dreams can."
                    —Joe Meno, author of *The Great Perhaps*

"Haunting . . . and poignant."   —*The Onion*

"Highly creative and beautifully strange."
                    —*Colorado Springs Independent*

"Jones's imagery and language invigorates a simple tale, bringing it to a fantastical place between poetry, drama, and delicate otherworldliness."   —*Willamette Week*

"Eerie, beautiful . . . incredible . . . a fantastic gem of a book."
                    —*Seattlest*

"Adept and flawless . . . Jones takes phrases and makes them into dreams and then folds those dreams in our pockets for safekeeping."   —*The Collagist*

PENGUIN BOOKS

DANIEL FIGHTS A HURRICANE

SHANE JONES (b. 1980) is the author of the novel *Light Boxes,* which was named an NPR Best Book of 2010. His poetry and short fiction have appeared in numerous literary journals, including *LIT, New York Tyrant, Fairy Tale Review,* and the *Milan Review.* He lives in upstate New York.

Daniel Fights
a Hurricane

A Novel

SHANE JONES

PENGUIN BOOKS

PENGUIN BOOKS

Published by the Penguin Group

Penguin Group (USA) Inc., 375 Hudson Street, New York, New York 10014, U.S.A.
Penguin Group (Canada), 90 Eglinton Avenue East, Suite 700, Toronto, Ontario, Canada
M4P 2Y3 (a division of Pearson Penguin Canada Inc.) Penguin Books Ltd, 80 Strand,
London WC2R 0RL, England Penguin Ireland, 25 St Stephen's Green, Dublin 2, Ireland
(a division of Penguin Books Ltd) Penguin Group (Australia), 250 Camberwell Road,
Camberwell, Victoria 3124, Australia (a division of Pearson Australia Group Pty Ltd)
Penguin Books India Pvt Ltd, 11 Community Centre, Panchsheel Park, New Delhi – 110 017,
India Penguin Group (NZ), 67 Apollo Drive, Rosedale, Auckland 0632, New Zealand
(a division of Pearson New Zealand Ltd) Penguin Books (South Africa) (Pty) Ltd,
24 Sturdee Avenue, Rosebank, Johannesburg 2196, South Africa

Penguin Books Ltd, Registered Offices:
80 Strand, London WC2R 0RL, England

First published in Penguin Books 2012

1   3   5   7   9   10   8   6   4   2

PUBLISHER'S NOTE

This is a work of fiction. Names, characters, places, and incidents either are
the product of the author's imagination or are used fictitiously, and any
resemblance to actual persons, living or dead, business establishments,
events, or locales is entirely coincidental.

ISBN 978-0-14-312119-0
CIP data available

Printed in the United States of America
Set in Chronicle Text G1 and Tungsten
Designed by Sabrina Bowers

ALWAYS LEARNING   PEARSON

For Melanie

Daniel Fights a Hurricane

Daniel began his day with a trip to a small gray building where he met a woman named Karen Suppleton, age thirty-seven.

Inside the building the windows cleared of clouds.

"Why are you here?" asked Karen Suppleton, who wore black stockings. Daniel thought they didn't fit with her title as a therapist. Her blouse, splashed with flowers.

"Oh, I don't know why I'm here, really. My wife thought it was a good idea?"

"Your wife—"

"She thought it would be a good . . . ummm, idea because of my anxiety. Things that I think."

Karen Suppleton had eaten two Hash Browns and a Sausage McMuffin with Egg that morning. She ate most of it in her car, alone, and finished the second Hash Brown at home. Daniel noticed the crumpled bag on a desk dominated by textbooks, pens, and scraps of paper.

"And what are those things?"

"Fear."

"Fear of . . . ?"

"I'm not sure this will help anything, but yeah, my wife wanted me to come here and talk about it, and I would do anything for her, and if she thinks it's a good idea, it probably is, right?"

"You can say as little or as much as you like. I'm not here to tell you your feelings."

"Right, so yes, I have this fear."

A ceiling fan turned but didn't generate air. Daniel asked if he could open the window, and Karen Suppleton said she would do it, that he should keep talking.

"It's just an overwhelming sense of dread, a complete and overpowering fear of something I can't place but feel throughout my entire body. It's in my veins, my blood. It's between my ribs. Sometimes I see it in forms."

From the open window, a cool breeze blew through the room, knocked the McMuffin bag on the floor, and for a brief moment Daniel imagined Karen Suppleton engaging him in a conversation about why a Sausage McMuffin with Egg was better than a Bacon, Egg & Cheese Biscuit.

"Fear and anxiety can stem from a variety of sources," said Karen Suppleton. "It's not unusual for us to place these fears in a living and breathing form."

Daniel looked out the window and thought about the pipeline he was working on. He went over the details in his mind—the broad flanges, the expansion tanks, elbows, tees, unions, and the water meter that broke an hour after being installed, setting the project back several hours.

"But this fear," continued Daniel, shifting in his seat, massaging his own shoulder with the opposite hand, feeling the breeze in his nostrils, "I see it as something completely else."

"You're very open and honest," said Karen Suppleton, feeling, with her tongue, a piece of Hash Brown between her back teeth.

"I see it as a Hurricane. I have these visions where this Hurricane comes through and tears open the sky and turns me, my wife, everyone I know, to trembling skeletons. I see it. I feel it. I've spent hours looking at the horizon."

"Interesting," said Karen Suppleton, who wrote in a three-subject red-covered notebook.

Daniel watched her write, but he couldn't see what she was writing.

"Interesting? That's it? That's all you have to say?"

"I'm listening to what *you* have to say, and it's interesting. Tell me more about the Hurricane."

"It's my fear. It's *the* fear. It's affecting my job, this building of a pipeline to the ocean, because I really think, as silly and crazy as it is, that a Hurricane could just pop up and erase everything."

Karen Suppleton wrote down the word "erase" and underlined it.

"And you're scared of dying from this Hurricane?"

He sat on his hands to stop them from shaking.

"I'm scared that my fear, my . . . ummm, yeah, imagination of this Hurricane, and everything it could bring, will become my reality. The visions I have—God, I'm surprised you don't think I'm crazy."

"You're smart. You're not crazy. I'm here to help you."

Daniel looked one last time at the greasy bag and felt

a deep sadness about it, the way it death-crawled its way across the floor toward the garbage can, being shoved by the breeze. He talked for another twenty minutes about the Hurricane, said good-bye to Karen Suppleton, paid a twenty-dollar co-pay when he didn't need to, and drove out to the job site, where three co-workers sat waiting with their faces turned up toward the sun, pipes scattered in a dirt field with a few corn husks.

Daniel Meets Iamso

The man with tattoos said there was someone I should meet. We walked through a corn-husk field, then through the town dimmed by evening sun. We arrived at a brick house gripped by vines that he called home.

In the distance the Hurricane snored against the horizon. My toes vibrated. The man with tattoos said to ignore it and opened the door.

Heard you recently lost your wife, said the man with tattoos as we walked into the belly of the house, me following, eyes darting from kitchen to living room and back to his trailing voice evaporating down a hallway.

She recently disappeared, I said.

The man with tattoos came back down the hallway. We stood in the kitchen, awkward to each other, his breath infused with mustard seed and grease. He wore a short-sleeved robe. A tattoo of our seaside town was visible on his exposed forearm.

The whistling of the Hurricane swept leaves off the roof and rained dirt down the windows. The man with tattoos filled a teapot with water and turned the stove on.

I have someone who can help, he said.

If it's a cop, then the answer is no, I said. A cop can't help me. They've already tried.

The man with tattoos poured the hot water into two cups, and we sat down at a wooden table carved with pictures of crashing waves.

Two bags of tea rose to the surface.

It's possible she's dead, I said. I hate to even think it, but it's a possibility.

It's not a cop, said the man with tattoos.

From down the hallway, where the man with tattoos had retrieved his robe, came a young boy, no older than eight or fourteen, difficult to say in such dim light. He wore overalls and held a pencil in one hand and a stack of papers in the other. I thought I saw a small knife tucked into his boot. He sat down at the table with us.

This is Iamso, said the man with tattoos. See, I told you he wasn't a cop.

The man with tattoos nodded toward Iamso, who wrote on a piece of paper.

I can tell you what you are feeling, said Iamso.

Over his brown-haired head and up slightly more, and then a little more, and up over the sink and through the window, I looked for the Hurricane.

Done, said Iamso.

He folded the paper in half and pushed it across the table with two fingers. The man with tattoos smiled like a magician. When I looked back at Iamso, a large glass of milk and some cookies were in front of him. I unfolded the paper.

Read it aloud, said Iamso.

> *There's an image of us as soldiers.*
> *You're gliding back, away from me,*
> *hands outstretched,*
> *wearing green fatigues,*
> *your mouth an open cannon,*
> *the floor black with night and full of stars.*
> *All around us, neon colors*
> *and trees with feathers falling,*
> *and you're gliding gliding,*
> *almost gone,*
> *your green fatigues a green parachute,*
> *and you're floating floating,*
> *and I'm only a lover of vintage pipes*
> *and not of ladders.*

Iamso finished his cookies and milk, a crescent of crumbs surrounding his glass. The man with tattoos, hands folded on the table, looked at me, his eyes wide as if he expected an answer.

Well, said Iamso, is that how you feel.

I suppose, I said.

You suppose, said Iamso.

He pushed his chair away from the table and ran back down the black mouth of hallway with the stack of papers tucked into his armpit.

I didn't mean to upset him, I said. Really, I do feel that way.

He's a writer of letters and poems, said the man with tattoos. Maybe much more. It's quite amazing. So on the spot and so fast.

Outside, the Hurricane slept. Beams of sunlight filtered through the window and created shadow pipes across the surfaces of the room.

I don't understand, I said. How does what he said help me.

The man with tattoos rolled his neck. On his throat a tattooed house leaned left, tilted backward, and slanted right. He yawned, and his jaw popped.

Well, you're responsible for the pipeline that will save our town, he said.

A week earlier I was asked to build a pipeline to the ocean for drinking water. As the only person in town who loves pipes and knows how to construct them, I said yes, bobbing my silly head back and forth saying yes, absolutely, yes, I can do that, sure, yes.

People keep talking about a Hurricane that creeps along the horizon, said the man with tattoos. He glanced out the window at the violet sky, the leaves. His shoulders wobbled.

I'm not sure what the Hurricane actually is, I said.

The man with tattoos ran his hand across his mouth, composed himself for a serious speech.

The rest of the way, take Iamso with you, he said. He has a great sense of direction. He can help you. He can tell you about yourself and write your feelings, stories. You shouldn't be alone out there, worried and sick, missing your wife, fear of the Hurricane holding you, not sleeping even for a short dream.

From down the hall, the metal clanking of pipes, Iamso running.

Slung over his shoulder, a huge burlap sack filled with blue pipes. Another bag contained sandwiches. He grabbed my hand and stretched my fingers toward the doorknob.

Come on, now, let's go, he said.

I allowed myself to be pulled out the door by Iamso. I waved to the man with tattoos, who tipped his teacup good-bye, and Iamso and I moved across the field of corn husks, small fingers popping the joints in my hands, guiding me through air as crisp as butchers' knives, pipes bouncing in a burlap sack, clanking wildly against one another, backbone, skeletal pain, a new beginning.

On the horizon the Hurricane tossed boats into a cloud-crowded sky.

Field of Horses

Daniel connected the smaller pipes until they reached the forest. From the last pipe, he thought he could smell the ocean, the home of the Hurricane, the water needed for their dying town.

Here is Daniel's drawing of the pipeline:

Here is how Daniel felt, according to a poem by Iamso:

> *Field of horses*
> *drag me through*
> *cracked tan, dust of clouds,*
> *dirt in a man's gums.*

Back home, Daniel packed a burlap sack with his favorite blue pipes. He flung the bag around his back and told Iamso he was ready.

They headed to where Daniel had stopped the previous day. Iamso wrote in a book as they walked. He told Daniel he was cataloging Daniel's feelings. Daniel went along with it, attempting to guess Iamso's age while trying to catch a glimpse of a sentence.

This will be great, said Iamso, and ran the spine of his book along the body of the pipeline as they walked.

When they came to the spot where the pipeline ended, Daniel threw his bag down, and the pipes flipped out in the form of a skeleton. Trees above lost their leaves with the wind. The line of blue pipes extended back into town, braced by chopped tree limbs. He could almost see the first pipes. Pipes so large you could walk through them. Daniel ran his finger around the open edge of the last pipe and wished for water. In the distance he thought he heard the Hurricane mumble.

I thought you said you were close, said Iamso, laying out his pipes in the form of an H, and then another H on top of that H, and so on.

I was, said Daniel. I thought I smelled salt.

He looked through the forest, to the ocean, but saw only the wind move trees.

Do you like my pipes, Iamso said. I made them into a ladder.

Iamso raised the set of H's and placed them against a tree. The feet of the top H rested on a branch lined with birds' nests.

You can climb it if you want. I prefer pipes to ladders, but you have to admit a ladder is handy, said Iamso, moving the ladder of H's made of pipes around until it was planted in the ground and clung to the branch. Go up and see how close we are to the sea.

Daniel went up the ladder. From the top he saw the ocean. On the horizon a barge carried a cloud.

We're pretty close, Daniel shouted before climbing back down.

Excited by the sight of water, he told Iamso they should get done as much as possible today. They'll spend the night here. The man with tattoos will be worried, but for now they'll work their way to the ocean. Soon everyone will have water from the pipeline.

The man with tattoos told me about your wife, said Iamso, who took down the ladder, disassembled it, and handed Daniel the first pipe to attach. I'm sorry, he said.

Maybe I'll find her, Daniel said.

They worked for six hours. All the small pipes became part of one large pipe shooting through the forest, aimed at the sea.

Iamso handed Daniel chunks of sandwich. Daniel attached pipes until it got too dark to see where the bolts went. They created a fire from the chopped tree branches that they didn't use during the day for braces on the line. Daniel's hands and face warmed from the flames. He imagined the sound of birthing waves. A tiger walked out from behind a tree, looked at him, then went back behind the tree.

I'll send a message, Iamso said.

From his book he tore out a piece of paper and wrote something. He folded the paper into a boat and placed it in the opening of the last pipe. Then, taking his canteen and feeding it into the mouth of the pipe, he poured some water underneath the little boat, and it disappeared down the pipeline, back to town.

A few minutes later, a paper fish was spit from the pipe. Iamso flicked the water off, unfolded it, read something, then crumpled it up and put it in his pocket.

Well, Daniel asked.

The man with tattoos thanks us for letting him know we are spending the night. He wishes he could send cookies and milk, but a paper fish isn't capable of carrying such things. Perhaps he should have folded a kangaroo. He says to get a good night's sleep if we plan to build more of the pipeline.

We probably have enough pipes for a half day's work tomorrow, said Daniel, looking at the deflated burlap sack, a bag clinging to a few pipes being pushed by the wind.

I'm ready for bed, said Iamso. See you in the morning.

Daniel couldn't sleep. He tossed and turned on his bed of leaves. He asked the tiger for a bedtime story. The tiger blinked his red eyes and went back to his tree.

Daniel thought about his wife, the way one foot was

slightly smaller than the other, enough so that she needed to buy two separate shoe sizes. He hummed a sleeping song and soon was asleep.

Iamso crawled over to Daniel, put his arm around his back, and slept against him.

Daniel dreamed of a hawk tearing apart the throat of a Hurricane, himself a giant who lifted up a leaf of sky to peek inside. He saw himself as a mongoose holding a rope in his teeth, running circles around the Hurricane, and then he met a group of men as tall and thin as trees. They threw neon-colored rocks into the ocean. When the rocks were gone, they found a large dial on the beach. They bent over and moved the dial to the right. The Hurricane buzzed, the clouds vibrated, and the wind slapped the ocean like a puddle into the sky. Everyone screamed, pointed at the sky. The tall men were running through the forest, bumping their heads on tree branches, and Daniel could hear Helena behind him, whimpering, but when he turned, he saw a little boy, his face scrunched up, wielding a green pipe over his head at the sea-sky ready to break.

Panic Attack

I am at the pipeline site run by Stuart Services LLC, a massive company with a logo resembling a candy cane vomiting water from the curved tip. My name is Daniel, thirty-two years old, and I possess what many would consider an irrational fear of a Hurricane lurking above, around, and inside me. This morning I attended a session with a therapist, a highly recommended woman named Karen Suppleton, who eats McMuffins, wears ripped black stockings, and smells of lilac, dish soap, and Hash Browns.

Once finished, ending at the Gulf of Mexico, the line will have spanned over 3,567 miles and have the capacity of pumping more than twelve hundred barrels of oil a day. A projected ending cost is roughly $45 billion, but it will most likely be much higher. I know this stuff because everyone here *has* to know this stuff before getting hired.

Few people know about my fear.

It was day four of work, and we were working on the second of six 16V32 crude-oil-fired engines, and I couldn't keep my eyes off the horizon. I was with Kevin DeLucia (a kind of shy guy who I always imagined had a secret hobby, like knitting late at night), Scott Ostrich (who had been divorced four times in two years), and John Diaz (a man unanimously known for his unfortunate "teeth" situation).

We worked for nearly six hours straight before thunder broke on my back. I collapsed. I writhed on the ground like a man on fire. Everyone stared at me until I composed myself enough to look up and see a cloudless sky.

"What the hell *was* that, man? I mean, shit, are you okay? Was that a stroke?" said Kevin.

"Maybe," I said, still trembling. My bones were rattles. "Yeah, a stroke."

"Get some help," said John. "Seriously, that was just . . . It was terrible, whatever it was. Your entire body was convulsing, and you were, like, spitting up your lunch."

I worked for another twenty minutes before excusing myself ("Gotta go to the bathroom," I said, or something like that) and ducking into one of the dozens of trailers—these ugly square white things, each with a ceiling fan that was never on.

Inside, I still felt like I was outside, under the cruel umbrella of the Hurricane. It felt like a wall moving toward me. I heard wind howling, and everything shook in a black-and-white blur. I splashed some water on my face. My heart stopped, I gasped, and it started up again. People outside yelled that they would miss the game if they had to work late.

I left early that day. My boss told me to visit a doctor, who couldn't find a thing wrong with me other than a slight heart murmur. I decided to call Karen Suppleton.

Karen

I received a phone call from my ex-husband, Daniel, saying he was scared and wanted to set up an appointment.

"I need help," he said. "I mean, I need professional help, and I want you to be the therapist."

When Daniel was at his worst, his voice trembled.

"I don't know," I said. "We've done this before, and I don't know if I can keep doing it. It's not healthy. You should see an actual professional."

"They'll think I'm crazy. I have visions that when the Hurricane hits, I'll be locked up in a padded room."

I told Daniel this would be the last time. I had done it before, setting the living room up like a psychologist's office, talking to Daniel in questions. When Daniel asked for help, when he begged for help, I wanted to be there for him no matter what.

"I need you to promise me that this will be the last time. Daniel, we're not married anymore. We're not together. I can't keep doing this. It's not fair to me," I said, clearing the coffee table of everything but a stack of magazines. "Do you understand that?"

"I do. Now, when can I schedule an appointment? Will there be a co-pay? Paperwork to fill out? I'm being very professional here," he said.

I smiled when I shouldn't have smiled. His voice was shaking. I told him to call back in two minutes.

The Story of Feelings Locksmith

In the morning I woke to Iamso hammering bolts into a new set of pipes. The sun was low, an angled yellow that hit the waists of trees and opened my eyes.

Iamso stood on a tree stump, pounding away, sparks flying. He wore an oversize pair of amber-tinted glasses. Where yesterday's ready-to-use pipes had lain was now a clean dirt floor. I walked to where Iamso worked, cracking branches and slipping through leaves as I went.

I wanted to get an early start, Iamso said, finishing up and jumping off the tree stump. This way we can spend more time talking.

I looked again, through the forest, but still couldn't see or smell the ocean.

What do my feelings have to do with anything, I asked.

Iamso sat down on a pile of leaves and wrote in his book. I remembered more grass from the day before. Now I saw only small patches drowned with dirt.

Here, said Iamso, handing me a paper.

> *Once, I smashed my teeth on rocks.*
> *Once, I climbed a tree*
> *to rescue a child stuck in a tree,*
> *my fingernails as claws bloodied.*
> *Where are you.*
> *Did you ever have that dream I had*
> *where the Hurricane*
> *throws you across the floor of the ocean.*

I looked up, and Iamso was eating a sandwich.

You should tell me more about your wife, he said. I could write about it as you talked.

Next to a tree, the one with the tiger from yesterday, a pile of feathers burned and smelled like singed hair.

We're building a pipeline, I said, so the town has a water supply.

Iamso wrote in his book and then placed the book inside his coat pocket.

One day, he said, the Hurricane will wake up. It could bring so much water that a pipeline for water will be pointless. I have visions of destroying the Hurricane. I have ideas on how to torture the Hurricane and these following images of being a hero for saving everyone.

I stomped the feather fire, but it wouldn't go out. I waved off the offer for water from Iamso. I asked him why the fire wouldn't go out. He shrugged.

You want to know my wife, I said. You want to know why she is missing, or gone, or whatever she is. I kicked the feather fire harder and harder.

Would it make you feel better if I told you a story about myself, said Iamso. Would that calm you down.

What. I guess it would, I said.

You guess.

It would, I said. Yes, I'd like that.

Iamso asked me to choose between two stories. One was called Feelings Locksmith; the other, World's Most Beautiful Man Has the World's Worst Teeth. I picked the first, because the second sounded too depressing for the morning. Iamso agreed and said he would tell me about him later, during moonlit hours when that story is best.

This happened when I was very young, said Iamso.

I looked for years in his face, tried to guess his age— ten, fifteen, maybe even younger than ten—I couldn't tell. He looked like someone who was hiding something awful inside him, or someone who kept secrets.

Most of us were farmer's children, said Iamso, and, like everyone in town today, our parents worried that the town would one day be destroyed by a Hurricane who lived on the horizon. So the school taught us how to construct tree houses, where the teachers predicted we would live. During my stay at the school, I was first nick-named Feelings. No surprise, really. I wrote poems and letters to everyone that echoed their feelings, even if they didn't want them. I couldn't help it. The biggest children swung for my jaw, and the teachers I crumpled to sobbing knees and elbows on the floor. The only person who liked me, who I could call a friend, was a boy named Squid.

Iamso stopped for a moment. A heavy wind seesawed the treetops. Feathers replaced leaves and fell. They moved down and through the air in half arcs. The burning pile grew. I didn't see the tiger.

We played this game, continued Iamso. There were two hundred rooms in the school, and Squid and I would run through each, slamming the doors behind us. It was fun. And then one night I ran into a room and closed a door and it locked. Just like that—clicked and locked for good. Squid was on the other side. It was awful. The door wouldn't unlock. The other doors in each room locked as well. All night I wrote poems and slid them under the door for Squid to read. He cried. I felt terrible. I felt like this.

Iamso flipped through his book and showed me a faded page.

> I can't open the door.
> I can't see you.
> The moon will break into three,
> and the sun will be there to miss the catch.
> I'm sorry.

The room I found myself locked into was full of pipes that ran across the floor and up the walls and around the ceiling, where they disappeared through hundreds of holes. I stepped around the pipes, crouched down, and touched them. Some were hot as coals, others cold as ice.

Mostly blue pipes with layers of rust. A few trembled with water rushing toward a teacher washing her hands up-stairs. I spent the night in this room, with Squid crying on the other side, until early morning, when a school janitor with a hipful of keys found us. And that wasn't the only time it happened. The locked doors followed me. Any-time I closed a door, it locked. I locked myself in the bath-room. I locked myself in classrooms. The janitor had to open my bedroom door each morning. My classmates nicknamed me Feelings Locksmith, which, if you think about it, is somewhat clever and absurd at the same time. It ended when I left school. I clearly remember the first day back home, closing my bedroom door and wrapping my fingers around the doorknob. The knob squeaked, clicked, and sprang open. I felt like I could breathe again. I felt a great rush of excitement. It was wonderful. And that's the story. We should head back into town for more pipes.

| 19

It's a good story, I said. Kind of sad, but good.

It's a funny story, said Iamso. You should feel good about yourself.

I almost asked what happened to his friend Squid but didn't. He was right that we needed more pipes. We de-cided to head back. As we walked, Iamso wrote in his book while humming a song and skipping every few steps.

Over there, on the other side there, said Iamso, look-ing up from his book. What's that.

The sun was high and yellow. A blotch of Hurricane breath evaporated against the blue sky in a white ring.

Not the sky, said Iamso. That man, walking toward us.

Moving across the field of corn husks was a tall man of blacksmith build. He wore brown pants and a tight-fitting, navy-colored, gold-buttoned coat. His hair was sandy and windswept, and as he got closer, we could see he had bright blue eyes, a carpenter-carved jawline.

It's him, said Iamso. The second story I wanted to tell you later. Not even close to moonlight. Odd how things work out.

We introduced ourselves. The man ran a hand through his hair. Iamso scribbled quickly in his book, then placed the book inside a coat pocket. I wondered how many pockets, how many pieces of paper and books were in that coat.

No need to introduce yourself, said Iamso. I know who you are, because I wanted to tell a story about you tonight, after we were finished working on the pipeline for the day.

The man stood still. He looked like he'd recently stepped from a hot bath, a fresh shave, a haircut, and a shampoo. I felt the grit of pipe rust under my nails, the sweat settle into the back of my neck.

I told him about the pipeline we were building to the ocean so the town didn't have to rely on the wells that are drying up. I told him about the constant fear of the Hurricane, even though it has never attacked, we don't think, and I don't believe it ever would, but our parents' parents believed so, and books had been written.

I rambled as his eyes narrowed. Iamso tugged on my sleeve like he was ringing a bell for me to stop.

A heavy sigh, and the man placed his hands in his

pockets. He looked at his feet. When he looked up again, he wiped tears from his eyes and tilted his head back to the sky. His lips trembled. From his pockets he revealed fists. Then his lips parted.

As his smile stretched toward his perfect ears, I noticed that nearly half his teeth were missing, and the ones remaining were made of wood, one of gold, one of stone, all jutting out in odd angles, his gums bloody and blackened. I couldn't see a tongue.

Hi, he said, extending his hand. I'm Peter.

Iamso placed a paper into my hand.

> *I'm not a monster,*
> *but the world's most beautiful man*
> *who also has the world's worst teeth.*
> *I'm so confused.*
> *Who isn't.*

Sorry about my smile, said Peter. It's my way of testing people. You didn't run away, so that's good. What's this about a pipeline.

He wrapped a faded blue handkerchief around his mouth and tied it behind his head. A triangle of fabric hung from his chin. He asked if the pipeline was for oil or water.

Water, I said. We're close to the ocean. I saw it before, but now I can't. We're on our way back to town for more pipes.

Peter swept his foot through a pile of corn husks. Can I ask you both a question.

I nodded. Iamso wrote something and handed the

book to Peter, who read it and smiled, the handkerchief rising slightly on his face.

Do you like caves. Especially warm caves containing some of the most beautiful pipes you'll ever see in your lifetime.

Is there a place like that, asked Iamso.

There is.

You have to show us, said Iamso, tugging on my sleeve so hard I thought the seams of my shirt would split.

Mean Bitches

Daniel finishes work and drives home. His knuckles are soldered black with grease and his mind alternates between Hurricane fear pulling him into the sky and the fact that *Oil rises from the soil at near boiling temperatures, then cools to a slight-burn when touched by the time it arrives at the first Pump Station through pipes that stretch across the land. The pipes are so large a man could walk through them.*

"Finally," says Darlene, the woman who is not his wife, who he wishes were his wife, who has lived with him for the past few weeks. A woman he met at work during an interview for a job promotion on the pipeline. "What took you so long?"

"I don't know. I don't think it took me any longer than usual to get home."

"Well, it was longer than usual. Hey, I want to tell you something."

Daniel thinks briefly about the pipeline snaking its

way through angry towns. The last town featured a group of drunken men who took turns shooting a rifle at the pipeline. They hit twice. Two eyeholes leaked oil. He thinks about the Hurricane, what it will look like (this time a tossed black blanket that disintegrates into rain). He sits on the couch, a brown recliner covered in patches of cat hair and bird feathers. He looks at Darlene, indicating she can begin her story.

"You won't believe what happened at work today." She sits next to him on the couch, pulls her feet up and under her ass, and squeezes his shoulder. "Hey, pay attention here, really, you're not going to believe this. Okay, so on my way to the bathroom, I always bring my water bottle to fill up at the water thing and leave it on one of the tables in the break room after I fill it up. So I go into the bathroom, and when I come out, I grab my water bottle and take a sip, and it tastes like soap." | 23

"What?"

"Soap. It tastes like someone put soap in the water. When I look at it, when I, like, tip the bottle to the side, I see these bubbles. And there's a sink in the break room and a big bottle of dishwashing soap, and I can see this little, like, dome of bubble coming from the top, like someone just used it. Someone, I don't know who, put soap in my water bottle. And not like a joke kind of thing either—no one has a sense of humor in my office. They don't pull pranks. And not one person said a thing in my office, not a single word when I told them."

"You confronted them about it?"

"Well, not really. I just mentioned that my water tasted funny, and of course they just ignored me."

"That's weird. I don't get it."

"Mean bitches."

"Right."

"I want to claw your eyes out."

"What?"

"I wanted to see if you were paying attention, because I didn't think you were. But this is important, to have someone in my office who wants to hurt me like that, and you don't really care. We need to have dinner. I'm thinking we cook up the chicken we've had in the fridge for the past week, if it's still good."

"Sounds good to me," says Daniel. "And I'm sorry that you had to go through that at work today. Is it okay if I take a quick nap?"

"Sure."

24 |

The bedroom is hardwood floors and white walls and reminds Daniel of a place he doesn't want to be, so he gets into bed and closes his eyes. The sky outside waits and, worse, watches. Chicken is cooked in a frying pan with oil and butter. He considers calling Karen, because she might have answers. There is something about Karen, something special, that Daniel feels in his bones. He imagines that she is someone he met in a previous life. There's more work to be done on the pipeline, cracked hard hats, bosses with megaphone voices, sweat on hands inside gloves making it difficult to twist the ends of pipes, and a Hurricane playing tag with Daniel's thoughts.

Box Built from Green Pipes

They followed Peter through the field of rotting corn husks—away from the forest, the pipeline, the town—and into a new forest lush with plants, green grasses, blooming flowers.

As a child, Daniel was told bedtime stories about children who walked into the caves and fell through to the opposite side of the earth.

Down a dirt path, he noticed multiple piles of feathers on fire. At the end of the path, a giant rock formation, a mouth, a tunnel of cool darkness flowing out and over them and up into the arms of the trees.

I thought it was a warm cave, said Iamso.

It is, said Peter, lighting a lantern. When we're deep enough inside where the pipes are, you'll see. It's something special.

Peter led the way into the cave, with Iamso in the middle and Daniel trailing. Daniel ran his fingers along the wet cave wall as he walked. After a few minutes, they stopped so Iamso could write. Daniel held the lantern.

It's not much farther, said Peter, adjusting his handkerchief. Maybe another ten minutes.

The heat from the ground, like fists, pounded the soles of their boots.

Here we are, said Peter.

He lit six lanterns that hung by ropes from the cave ceiling. Writing covered the cave walls in bright colors, mostly pictures of animals, a few words in bubbled letters that Daniel couldn't make out. In the center of the opening where they stood was a huge box, a square, built from green pipes. The outside of the box consisted of pipe ladders, which Peter used to climb to the top of the massive structure.

This, he said from the top where he stood, is made from very expensive pipes. It's very special. His voice reached a needle-pricked pitch in his excitement.

Peter stayed on top of the box for a few minutes before climbing back down. Iamso wrote furiously. Peter told Daniel to climb to the top of the box so he could show him something.

The pipes were warm and had rust scabs that Daniel picked off during his ascent. Bats flew over and disappeared into a black ledge.

Once Daniel was atop the box, Peter asked if he was ready, and Daniel said he was, although he had no idea what that meant. He felt ready for anything. His wife was missing. He had been with her one day and she was gone the next, and he couldn't remember what she looked like. He remembers helping her pack her bags, a living room with a fallen floor lamp, the light spilled across the carpet, her face and name hazy, and she said she couldn't be married to someone like him anymore.

A faucet, a little wagon-wheel shape attached to the cave wall, Peter squeaked to the left. A hose ran from the little wagon wheel, down the cave wall, and across the floor, until it reached the box Daniel sat atop.

Daniel felt each pipe below him fill with water. Under his thighs warm water rushed through the vintage metal. The entire shape, this mad contraption constructed who-knows-when and who-knows-why, woke up, shook with rivers. Pipes as pumping veins pressed into Daniel's skeleton. His hands wrapped around pipes as limbs. His arms vibrated as the shape vibrated, and Daniel smiled.

What's the point of this, he shouted to Peter, who kept a hand on the leaking faucet.

I don't know, he yelled back. I just think it's beautiful.

Maybe it has no point, said Iamso.

That's what I just said, yelled Peter. It's beautiful, and that's all there is to it.

After Iamso took a turn, then Peter, and Daniel once more, they sat on a rock and ate some sandwiches. Daniel stared at the box, trying to understand who had built it and why. And why run a pipeline into a cave. Or was the water itself from the cave. Maybe there were rivers nearby. Had someone else, a thousand years ago, run a line to the ocean because of a drought.

Can you drink the water, Daniel asked. Is it salty.

It tastes like salt, Peter said. Don't know how, but I imagine it's somehow connected to the ocean.

Peter asked Iamso what he was. Daniel told Peter he could write a poem expressing how anyone felt. Iamso finished his sandwich in two bites, wrote a poem, and then handed it to Peter, who smiled, the handkerchief rising. He bit his lip and agreed that yes, it was exactly true.

Daniel wondered if they had enough time to gather more pipes back in town. Most likely not. Although he was glad to meet Peter, to discover the box, they had lost daylight. Sitting there in the cave, he thought about the ocean, what waves looked like up close, magnified. He felt the more pipes they attached, the farther they moved from the ocean.

We should go, he said. Thanks for showing us this.

What do you think, said Peter, the chances are of the Hurricane waking up.

Daniel shrugged. I have no idea, he said.

Very possible, said Peter. A man named Harold told me that the Hurricane has flooded the sky before.

Is that true, said Iamso. Are you joking.

Peter took a deep breath. A wet spot formed on his handkerchief where his mouth was. Yes, it's true, he said. So much water was in the sky that it rained for a month.

They finished their sandwiches, and Peter asked if it was possible to work on the pipeline at night. Daniel said it was, with proper lighting. Peter pointed to the lanterns and showed Daniel a knife.

But we'll need more pipes, he said. It will take at least an hour to get back into town and then another hour—

I have pipes here, said Peter. Hundreds.

Iamso took the knife from Peter. He ran in a circle, jumping up and cutting down the lanterns, catching each one as he landed on his feet.

Air Gauze

Daniel doesn't go to work on the pipeline. Instead he sits in his car, in a Target parking lot, and calls Karen Suppleton. A woman tells Daniel he has an appointment in two weeks, but this isn't good enough, because he needs to talk to someone now, and Darlene won't do, because she's only a woman he recently decided to live with. He can't talk to her. She doesn't know him like Karen knows him. He tried this morning, but she was playing music and dancing, and it all felt dreamy, the air like gauze he moved through on his way to the car, and now this Target parking lot.

Karen can fit him in at twelve-thirty, says the woman, who sounds just like Karen. Daniel says okay and sits in his car for the next three hours before driving over. He falls asleep and has a dream where he and Karen Suppleton are in bed eating bowls of pasta. They are watching television. Hanging from the ceiling by ropes are different-size pipes. In the dream Daniel asks why she is there in bed and asks where his wife is. Karen Suppleton says that she is his wife. Daniel stands on the bed and hits a few of the pipes so they swing around, and then he gets back into bed and finishes his pasta. Karen Suppleton kisses him and tells him that she is going to leave him if he doesn't get better, and right before Daniel wakes up, he says to her, "But that's why I'm coming to see you, to get help. This pasta is delicious."

"This isn't an emergency really," says Daniel, sitting down across from Karen Suppleton. "I just needed to talk to someone. I'm surprised I could actually come in today."

Karen Suppleton wears the same outfit she wore during their first appointment. Daniel looks, but there is no McMuffin bag. Outside, a rally, a protest of some sort, moves in a circle around a pool of water in front of a building. Two people dressed in clown costumes have large $ symbols painted on their backs.

"I leave open spots throughout my day for this sort of thing," she says. "It's actually my lunch break."

"I didn't sleep last night."

"And what kept you up? Were you thinking about the Hurricane?"

Karen notices how thin Daniel appears. He's grown a beard and gotten a haircut. His brown eyes are dark, and she rarely makes contact with them.

"I was. I kept thinking about how I know it's not real, this idea of a Hurricane coming and just destroying everything, but in a way it *could* be real, right? Nothing says that it won't happen. Weather is unpredictable. And my job, where I'm working on this pipeline, we're basically moving it closer and closer to the ocean, and the fear is that once it hits the ocean, the Hurricane will become a reality. I stayed up all night thinking about what's real and what isn't. Sometimes I can't tell the difference."

"Do you think this moment is real?" She puts her legs up on a coffee table crowded with books.

"I think so. I can feel it. I know I'm here."

"You think the Hurricane is real?"

"I do. Why would I be thinking about it so much if it weren't real in some way? But I also know it's crazy to think that something like that would happen. Then again, I know I'm going to die, right, and I don't know when that's going to happen. So the Hurricane can be real, too."

"Well," says Karen Suppleton, taking her legs off the

coffee table. "Death is a truth, a reality that we all will experience. The idea of the Hurricane is just that, an idea in your imagination. It's not definite in the future the way death is."

Daniel looks out the window. One of the clowns with a $ symbol painted on his back throws a rock through a window. The crowd cheers.

"It's a state office building," says Karen Suppleton. "And please, just call me Karen from now on."

"Okay."

There's an awkward silence before Daniel remembers a dream he had the night before. Karen asks him to explain the dream. He says he saw a group of men, including himself, building a pipeline to the ocean. Not where he works, but a different pipeline. He talks about the pipeline for nearly forty-five minutes, ending with the Hurricane using an ax to cut it open, an oily mist goose-bumping the sky.

"It was one of those dreams," he said, "that feel real after you wake from it."

Fog Face

I had a terrible, clear dream. The Hurricane shoved the ocean depths up the beach and chased deer, who reached for the edges of the forest. Hurricane as bully. Hurricane as the death of me and my wife. Hurricane as bloodied sky. Hurricane inching closer to our throats.

Iamso helped Peter hang the lanterns at the end of tree limbs they had stabbed into the dirt. The glowing lights lined the path where the pipeline would soon go.

Maybe it's going to come, I said. Maybe it has before. Maybe that's when my wife went missing.

I didn't know who I was talking to, because no one was paying attention.

Easy, said Peter, who now wore a black handkerchief with white crosses that ran across his mouth. The Hurricane may be a myth, he said. No one has ever seen a Hurricane.

The lanterns were set. I put on a pair of goggles and started hammering bolts. Sparks flew, and I became my own lantern as the pipeline grew. Cinders seared into the spaces between the hairs on my forearms. Iamso cleaned the burns with a dry cloth. Peter worked the lanterns, moving them along with the extending line.

We pushed forward, to the ocean.

I told Peter and Iamso I needed to see something, to wait a few minutes. I said, Iamso can keep working on the line.

I took a lantern and walked through the woods. I stepped on branches, leaves, patches of blue-black grass and around piles of burning feathers that smoked a skyward funnel. When I couldn't hear Iamso and Peter, I ran to where I thought the ocean was. Faster, I hurdled fallen trees, zigzagged up and over shaggy-haired rock gardens. I yelled for the ocean. I pushed myself into a sprint, through a clearing in the woods, and I just needed to see it, the horizon and its smeared ocean. I tripped, stumbled. A bear throwing acorns like grenades at squirrels told me to slow down, *There is no hurry in this life, because everything will be okay*, he said, but I had to hurry, because there it was—yes yes yes the ocean.

I stopped, chest at my throat, and what I thought was the ocean was a cloud, a rolling fog that moved faster than I could run. It came down and seeped through me and headed toward the unfinished pipeline.

The sky darkened by double because the sky folded in on itself.

When I got back, Iamso leaped from the tree stump, and I stepped up and hammered two bolts to finish. Water dripped from the last finished pipe, and a paper canoe fell from the edge.

It doesn't say anything, said Iamso, splitting the sides of the canoe open. He held the wet paper, its corners pulp, up to the lantern light.

I've seen that before, said Peter. Carved into a tree.

Any idea what it means.
No, no idea, said Peter.
So who sent it, asked Iamso.
The man with tattoos may know, I said. We'll ask him about it tomorrow.

We used every pipe that Peter had offered us and fell tired. I smelled like cave. The three of us huddled around the campfire. Iamso was the first to fall asleep. Peter pulled down his handkerchief, slowly, as if he only had heard from villagers, and not seen, the ugliness of his own mouth. He held a pocket mirror with one hand and with his other hand took out a wooden-handled tooth-brush from a bag. His mouth open wide, he brushed the few back teeth and the black holes that were his gums. Blood and yellow pus ran down his chin. He was forced to smile when he went for the front teeth. The most beauti-ful man in the world with the worst teeth in the world, Peter cried and brushed his teeth in the glow of the fire. The fear of the Hurricane whispered through our hair. Through our teeth. The trees were scared of wind.

After Peter fell asleep, his mouth stuffed with white cotton, and Iamso broke into a repetitious snoring, I crawled to where Iamso dreamed.

I pulled a book from his coat pocket. It had a green cover, and on the first page it read:

I could have saved you.

On the next page:

Dreamed I built a pipeline
with a young boy named Iamso
and the world's most beautiful man
who had the world's worst teeth.
Helena, I've thrown a rope and anchor through the moon.
I could have saved you.

And the next:

> *I ran toward the ocean in a mad dash but only found*
> *a cloud.*

And the next page:

> *I, too, felt like an animal*
> *right before sleep,*
> *a hawk tearing open the throat of a Hurricane,*
> *then a mongoose holding a rope*
> *in its teeth*
> *running circles around the Hurricane,*
> *and then I was asleep*
> *and dreaming of people as tall and thin as trees.*

On the next page:

> *When is sleep a coma.*

And the next:

> *I lost you in a Hurricane.*
> *Our town wasn't prepared.*
> *I was taken out to sea and fell asleep there.*
> *Later, the tall men asked me questions,*
> *and I created a dream*
> *where there was a foggy morning*
> *with horses eating grass and—*

Please don't read my book, said Iamso, his hand a tight circle around my wrist.

He didn't look angry, but disappointed. I slowly

moved back to where my blanket and bags were. I thought, A tent or a tipi would have been a good idea.

Later, and I was finally dreaming. My eyes closed around a grassy field in the distance, where a group of horses grazed. A pond held fog. Iamso sat on a rock. Peter danced, his feet kicking outward, his hands covering his mouth. The sky dripped ukulele. Music could be heard. The pipeline wrapped itself around the sun.

Job Termination

They say, We're letting you go, and I tell them a Hurricane will throw their silly pipeline (I comment on the diameter of the first pipes, so large that people could live in them) into the sky, and they say, Daniel, you see, this is why we are letting you go.

I sit in my car for an hour, daydreaming disaster.

In the backseat is a half bag of bread, work clothes, bottles of water, books provided by Stuart Services on pipeline construction, and a jar of peanut butter. I have a moment that everyone has, and that moment is wondering if I'm crazy or not. The answer is no. I'm simply going through something, and I need to get away and clear my head. I need to fix myself, and it would help if I had my wife back, who has left me because she has had too many moments where she's wondered if I'm crazy or not.

I drive to a nearby ATM and check my bank account. The screen reads, $2,379.82. I take out half.

Then I drive parallel with the pipeline. Driving because I'm getting away from what is back there. Driving because I'm running away from the Hurricane.

Elbows as Horns

The first pipes were built in a large concrete building. It was here that the dream of water would appear and flow into a salt-filtering basin. With diameters larger than a tall man, the pipes extended through a chiseled-out concrete wall, away from the town, and slightly decreased in width until a single person could manage them when they entered the forest. You could carry them in burlap sacks, they were so small.

Back in town, people stand on ladders and hold magnifier pipes against their eyes. Daniel stops a woman in the street and asks what they are doing. The woman tells Daniel they are Hurricane watchers, watching for the Hurricane, obviously.

I've never heard of that before, he says. Something new.

The woman says she has already said too much, she needs to leave, and, lowering her head, runs off.

The Hurricane watchers scan from left to right and back again. The women wear silk dresses, most in black. The men wear brown canvas button-down shirts tucked into steam-pressed corduroy pants.

Maybe this means it will happen, says Peter as they walk through the town.

The Hurricane will bloat our faces with salt water and death, thinks Daniel.

This morning, shouts a woman Hurricane watcher, I saw the Hurricane roll onto its side.

When a breeze moves through the town, it lifts Peter's handkerchief, and Daniel sees a wooden snaggletooth.

Townsfolk board up windows. Walls are drawn and created from stacks of bags filled with dirt. The bags of dirt encircle homes and the concrete building that cradles the first pipes. A scream chases clouds from the sky. The Hurricane watchers all look up.

The few remaining clouds are shredded with claw marks.

Some of the townsfolk toss the final bags of dirt into place and run into their homes. Others collapse into rocking and drooling fetal positions. They moan to the scream that trails, fades, dissipates from the sky. Iamso asks what's happening.

That was him, a Hurricane watcher says. That was the Hurricane.

Where, asks Iamso. I didn't see anything. Are you lying about it. I never lie about anything, because it hurts people.

In the sky, says the woman, who looks through her magnifier pipe, aims it back toward the horizon. What just happened has happened twice this week.

Peter is in a crouched position, his knees wide apart, elbows as horns extended from his buried head. He's trembling. He says the Hurricane will soon wake up.

Daniel places a hand on Peter's shoulder and guides him to his feet. He tells him the Hurricane is more death-myth than death-storm, and before he can elaborate, the man with tattoos comes up the street, shoulder-splitting his way through the crowd.

The man with tattoos says he has something that everyone needs to see. There's a long pause, and finally Daniel says, Okay then, what is it.

The man with tattoos rolls up his sleeve and reveals a new tattoo, which reads, *HURRICANE ♥ YOU*, in thin black scroll, a blue carved-wood-style wave beneath.

Look, he says. Isn't it interesting. Isn't it really something. I mean, no one has anything like this.

Daniel says they need more pipes. They're close. He introduces Peter, who tries to stop shaking.

The man with tattoos shows them the *HURRICANE ♥* *YOU* tattoo again. He displays his arm like a serving dish plated with bread and jam. When the group says nothing, Daniel just wanting an answer for more pipes, the man with tattoos places his forearm under Daniel's nose.

It's good, says Daniel.

Then the man with tattoos looks at Peter. Most likely, he says, you are the most beautiful man ever.

Peter reaches behind his head to untie the handkerchief, his arms and elbows blocking the dull sun behind him. A half crown of women stand near, watching, whispering. Peter loosens the knot. The handkerchief falls down his throat and rests on his shoulders. His lips part to fungus and rot.

Truly hideous, says the man with tattoos, watching the women run away. Okay, let's talk about getting you guys more pipes.

They walk to a nearby teahouse, the Bird's Nest, and order a pot of blackberry tea. Iamso leaves the table, is seen outside the window talking to a Hurricane watcher, then comes back inside and writes in his book. Peter and the man with tattoos talk card games. Daniel slides his teacup back and forth between his hands, waiting for the tea. When he turns to get some change from his coat hung on his chair, he notices a picture carved into the wall:

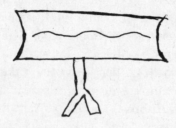

Can someone tell me what this means, he asks of no one in particular.

He hears the pouring of the tea, turns back around to find the waitress filling each cup.

When she pours the last cup, the man with tattoos' cup, he raises his newly tattooed arm to her eyes and waits for her to comment. She says nothing. She double-checks that each teacup is filled to the brim and leaves the remainder of the pot in the center of the table before walking away to the bar area.

You didn't send a paper with that symbol through the pipeline, asks Daniel.

No, says the man with tattoos. I've never seen that before.

The teahouse fills with people. It's raining outside. Someone complains that his shirt is covered in Hurricane spit.

So how close are you to the ocean, asks the man with tattoos.

Close, says Peter. We must be.

Conversations swirl around them.

Have you actually seen the ocean, someone asks.

Not yet, says Iamso.

Someone says, I feel like I'm living in a coma.

You there, more tea.

I haven't gotten a first cup of tea.

A child says, The Hurricane is a garbage collector.

The man with tattoos tells Daniel that their last well is almost empty. They measured yesterday. There's enough water for a week or so, but not more.

Daniel remembers when the town bloomed with full wells. Beautiful wide wells, stone-crowned, sprouting moss, ivy-encrusted. He remembers water filled with light pulled up in a wooden bucket. He remembers the wells drying up, and the idea, the first sketches, to run a pipeline to a water source. Groups of five assembled and looked for lakes, overgrown puddles, fat streams, and new rivers. Everyone knew that an ocean was out there, but not how far. The Canary brothers, wielding pickaxes and shovels, wanted to be heroes. They rope-climbed to the bottom of one well. They dug for a week straight, hoping their boots would be glued to mud, bubbling water inches beneath. The Canary brothers grew so weak they had to be pulled via rope and harness up the well by a group of five who had returned with the sad taste of dry forest on their tongues. Someone asked when it had rained last. Then they prayed for rain. Then they worried they had prayed too hard and the Hurricane would answer. They looked to the horizon for answers.

Maybe even two weeks, says the man with tattoos. The last well is quite large.

Peter shivers and mumbles that the Hurricane will drown everything. Seeing the town, the Hurricane watchers unsteady on their ladders monitoring the horizon, has twisted him. Daniel thinks maybe Peter was one of the originals who prayed for rain but decides not to ask him.

I'll help you load more pipes, says the man with tattoos. Someone bumps into his elbow, causing him to spill some tea. But you should probably see the last well first, to give you perspective on what we're dealing with here.

Tipi

The first call I get isn't from my wife, but from Karen Suppleton, who tells me if I intend to schedule another appointment to do it soon. She wants to see me. I tell her there won't be another appointment. I'm walking the aisles of a Dick's Sporting Goods store, picking out camping equipment.

"We've made progress, Daniel. It wouldn't be such a great idea to just suddenly stop. I wanted to talk more."

"Maybe when I get back," I say. "I just need some time

for myself. I won't suddenly stop. I'd like to talk to you more."

I purchase a tent that looks like a tipi for $44.99, a canteen for $9.99, and a flashlight that is free with my first two purchases. At the checkout the man in front of me buys one twenty-pound weight, asks for a bag, and carries it out to his car, his right side leaning.

After I leave Dick's Sporting Goods, I drive to a nearby coffee shop and sit and drink coffee. Will people worry about me? Will my wife ask questions? Am I a coward for doing this?

I drive as far away as possible from work, where the pipeline resides and grows by the day.

I will go to the forest, away from the ocean, away from the Hurricane, away from the horizon.

Tonight I will put together the tipi and live inside it | *43* with a little light and call it my home.

Dying Wells

The man with tattoos lowers a lantern by way of rope into the last well. He says he doesn't give a shit if the lantern smashes against the well wall or if he drops the rope and the lantern is lost forever.

I lean over the stone side to the last well, the stomach of my shirt instantly stained with dirt and moss. I wait for the bottom to appear. When it does, the water is a quiet slick black. The lantern dips in and unfolds ripples, and the man with tattoos tells me to notice how clear the water is. Then he lowers the lantern into the shallow depths until it rests on a floor that now glows.

I see two fish asleep in what they think is a corner. The light flickers, and the man with tattoos pulls the lantern back up until his hand touches a wet section of rope, whereupon he swings the lantern up into the air and it crashes behind us.

I caught you checking out my new tattoo, he says.

There's not much water left at all, I say. If we can carry enough pipes, we'll see if we can reach the ocean tomorrow.

I don't tell him about the vision I had while walking out here: the ocean extending its arms and legs into the forest, then obliterating itself into a flood.

How can you not know how close you are.

I answer, Yesterday I thought I could smell salt in the air, but I couldn't see the ocean. I'm just not sure.

I walk from the well and past Iamso, who feeds a chipmunk scraps of bread. A little farther away, near some bushes, Peter talks to two women who followed us here, or rather followed Peter. One of them brushes his arm with a finger and can't stop smiling.

Before I can tell Peter we'll be leaving soon to gather more pipes, the woman says to him, I want your face.

The other says, I want your mouth.

Peter says something, hand over handkerchief, and walks a few steps from them. He tells me we need to go. He says one of the women told him a baby died of thirst this morning. Peter has tears in his eyes, and the mouth of his handkerchief is blood-soaked.

Daniel Waits for the Dark

Daniel parks his car on the side of the road and walks into the forest. He looks for the Hurricane in the sky. When he doesn't see it, he thinks it, creates an image of a flood folding itself inside another flood, feels it move down his spine until it pushes him from his car, up into the woods, walking a new path to where he has decided to live for a while.

He leaves his cell phone in the car.

Daniel walks for nearly four hours, stepping around piles of burning feathers and ignoring the tiger that seems to follow. He sweeps his boots through leaves, grass, weeds, broken trees wet with rain, nearly trips on a pipe stabbed in the dirt.

When he enters a clearing, he makes his tent that looks like a tipi and gathers wood for a fire. He carves a picture into a tree from boredom. He sits next to the pile of wood and waits until dark so it can become a fire.

Karen

I'm at the grocery store standing in the bread aisle when my neighbor, an extremely thin woman named Allison, turns the corner and waves. She speed-walks up to me, heels clicking, says hello, and asks about Daniel.

"I think he's okay," I say. "Honestly, I'm not sure how to deal with it sometimes. I want to help and want to run away, and that doesn't make sense at all does it? No, it doesn't."

"It must be hard," says Allison, grabbing a loaf of multigrain bread and tossing it into a handcart containing a dozen yogurts. "If I were you, I don't know what I would do. We should have lunch sometime so we can talk about it, if you want."

"Oh, I think everything is fine," I say. "I'm sure Daniel is okay, wherever he is."

"You don't know where he is?"

"Right now, not exactly. He may have gone camping. Maybe hiking at Red Ridge Mountain, which is something we did together often. Really, I'm sure he's okay."

I tell Allison that lunch would be nice, and she smiles and gives me a hug, and she tells me about a yoga class that really helps with her stress. The chances of Allison and me having lunch are slim, because we've never done that before. It's only something she says for comfort.

I walk to the produce section. All along the wall are green leafy vegetables, yellow summer squash, purple-headed cauliflower. For a moment I think of never speaking to Daniel again, that he is not my problem, and I feel strong but terrible. Under the awning where the lights are that showcase the produce is a water system that clicks on. A thin mist wets the vegetables. There's a mini sound system that plays thunder. A child standing in a shopping cart shouts, "Thunderstorm, Mom! Umbrella time!" I put my hand into the mist and grab broccoli, letting little bubbles of water layer my skin.

The Two-Second Dreamer

These were the final pipes, and we could carry hundreds. The man with tattoos helped us fill burlap sacks until they poured from the opening. One bag was bolts. Another sandwiches. Iamso offered to write me another poem, but I was too concerned with the pipeline, daydreaming ocean surf around my ankles. Soon we would feed the pipeline into the ocean so we could have water.

We walked across the field of corn husks and into the forest, where the end of the pipeline sat open and waiting to be finished.

Several invisible sections of pipeline ahead, a man who was lying on the ground stood up. He approached us and introduced himself as a two-second dreamer. He wore a button-up shirt with cutoff sleeves and ocean-colored pants. His boots were mud-colored. He was young, but with gray hair and a mustache.

Iamso showed me what he wrote in his book. It read, *I can't write anything about this person.*

Before you start your work, would anyone like to buy a two-second dream, the dreamer asked. I know you're busy, especially if this pipeline is headed to the ocean, which I bet it is, but it looks like everyone here could use one. It's very fast, and you'll feel much better and work harder.

Can we pay you in sandwiches, asked Iamso.

The two-second dreamer nodded and said yes, he hadn't eaten in days.

Then we'll take three, said Iamso. One for each of us.

Peter handed over three parchment-wrapped sandwiches. The sky shook with Hurricane-speak.

The two-second dreamer emptied his bag containing a bird-beak-yellow pillow and a green wool blanket. He lay on the corn-husk field's floor as if it were a bed, propped his pillow under his head, and pulled his blanket from his feet to his chin. He kicked off his boots, then wiggled until comfortable, a smile pressing into the pillow.

All right, he said. Get ready.

Iamso moved a corner of blanket over the two-second dreamer's exposed foot.

You'll be first, said the two-second dreamer, leaning up slightly to see Iamso.

Again Iamso tried to write something but this time ended up sketching a field of horses and a farmer holding a palmful of blueberries. He shrugged and put his book inside his coat pocket and waited for his two-second dream.

Before falling asleep, the two-second dreamer unwrapped one of the sandwiches and took a large bite. A strong breeze blew across the field, low and at our knees. The two-second dreamer said it was only the Hurricane whistling, dreaming of blowing out a candle on his night-stand.

Sorry, said the two-second dreamer, spitting crumbs. Here we go.

His head fell into the depths of his yellow pillow, his eyes shut, his mouth closed, then parted into a little open pipe I imagined water could come from.

Only seconds passed. His eyes flicked open. He tossed the blanket from his body and stood. He cupped a hand over Iamso's ear and whispered. Iamso's eyes broke to puddles. He took out his book and wrote something he wouldn't show me.

Thanks, said Iamso. That was a good two-second dream.

All right then, said the two-second dreamer. Who wants next. You there, good-looking. He pointed to Peter, who was holding up a hand mirror, peeling a thin layer of blood from a front tooth. You're next. First let me take another bite of sandwich.

As the two-second dreamer ate, I noticed something on the horizon and walked to it.

Iamso called my name, but I waved him off. A hundred yards or so from Peter, Iamso, and the two-second dreamer, I took from my bag a magnifier pipe.

On the horizon a ladder rested against the sky. Someone was at the top of the ladder, moving a cloth back and forth as if cleaning a teahouse or shop window. The person turned. He saw me. He waved his cloth into my magnifier pipe. I waved back and then lowered the magnifier pipe from my eye.

When I returned, Peter was laughing and covering his mouth with both hands. A tooth fell from behind his fingers. He picked it up off the ground and placed it in a pants pocket.

That was a hilarious dream, he said.

The two-second dreamer looked at me and asked if I was ready. I said I was. He lay back down, placed his head on the pillow, and pulled the blanket to his chin.

Two seconds later he woke. He stood up and cupped

a hand around my ear and whispered, The dream was you living inside a pipe, underwater. An entire town flooded. People lived on the floating roofs of their homes. Others were inside the pipe, with you, in lantern light, living their normal lives.

I was inside a pipe, I asked. But how.

It's only a dream, said the two-second dreamer, stepping away from me. It was a very large pipe.

Was everyone okay, I asked. Will everything be okay.

Yes.

Was my wife there.

I didn't see your wife there, no.

Behind the two-second dreamer's shoulder, Peter retied a new handkerchief around his face, and behind Peter the sky was stained with Hurricane breath. That man on the ladder, I thought, must be in charge of cleaning the stains from the sky.

50 |

If you don't mind, I'd like to work with you, said the two-second dreamer. I have nowhere to go. I can pay everyone in two-second dreams and help build the pipeline. Please.

Absolutely, said Iamso. We could use a fourth.

A walking and winding tail of us four, our makeshift family, moved along the pipeline.

Daniel Living in the Woods, a Blending of Worlds

I'm alone until the man with tattoos comes into the light of the fire. He comes from somewhere deep in the woods, way out here, where I thought I was by myself trying to forget about the Hurricane.

Mind if I sit with you and get some warmth, he says, crouching down on the dirt, hands as a shield.

Where did you come from.

I'm working on a pipeline, he says, sitting down and crossing his legs, hands still held out to the fire. I just can't work on it anymore today. I needed to get away.

I was working on that pipeline, too, I say.

On his right arm, a tattoo of a seaside town complete with curling ocean and tin-roofed shacks. On his other arm, words I can't make out. There's a house inked up his throat.

I didn't see you out there, he says. Not sure how close we are to the ocean.

I thought about shooting off some calculations. I imagined drops of oil caught in a breeze becoming a black net that covered skyward-looking deer.

You're close, I say.

The man with tattoos stayed for a while. He said I wasn't missing much at the pipeline, but they could use my help. I said I didn't want to go back, because that's where the Hurricane would hit.

Isn't the Hurricane more myth than reality, he asked before leaving.

Guess we'll find out, I said.

Karen

I'm worried about Daniel, because I understand how fragile his mind is. For Daniel, having a job is important, because it keeps his imagination distracted. Without the distraction it gives him more time to think, deepens the fantasy. Part of me wants to get closer to him, and another part of me wants to distance myself.

Tonight I do something to comfort myself that I've done since college: I drive to the store and buy three large bottles of carbonated water. When I get home, I put all three in the freezer for thirty minutes. The flavors are: lemon, lime, and cranberry. Once they're cold enough, I sit on the couch with all three bottles lined up on the coffee table and watch the bubbles rise from the bottom to the skinny necks. I turn on the television and find the most mindless reality show and for the next two hours drink all three bottles of carbonated water. There's something about the fizzy feeling of carbonated water that relaxes me. Even when I open the third bottle and the water froths over my hand in fizzle and wets the carpet, I don't mind. I enjoy it all. I drink and watch people on TV argue and eat and cry in the backseats of taxis. The routine of carbonated water calms me. I still wonder where Daniel could be and what he is thinking.

Canoe-Shaped Coffin

The two-second dreamer asks Daniel about his wife. He says she's missing. He asks Daniel if he'd like a two-second dream for her, and Daniel says no.

Why not, asks the two-second dreamer. It won't take long. I'll whisper it to you, and if you see her again, you can tell her. You can save it.

Daniel imagines Helena in a canoe shaped and painted like a coffin. She's out in the middle of the ocean, standing up in the canoe, waving a white flag. Then she lies back down in the canoe, and it just looks like a coffin floating on the water, headed to the horizon, where it will fall off.

Okay, he tells the two-second dreamer. Why not. Peter and Iamso get smaller as they walk ahead. He waves for them to go on.

The two-second dreamer lies on the ground, falls asleep instantly, and wakes moments later. He stands and whispers the dream for Helena.

Will you remember it, asks the two-second dreamer.

Yes, says Daniel. It's one of the most beautiful dreams I've ever heard. I can see it.

As they walk, the two-second dreamer asks about Iamso, and Daniel tells him he can write a poem that shows a person's feelings. The two-second dreamer brushes bruised bird feathers from his shoulder and says the Hurricane is playing Tear Apart a Bird's Nest—a cruel and twisted game.

We need to catch up, he says. Let's have a race, what do you say.

What.
To catch up to them.
A race.
Yes, a race.
I'm not rea
Go.

Daniel Imagines the Opening of Joints

When the Hurricane hits, crystal towers filled with rats will break apart like glaciers. A pipeline will lift from a trench, and four thousand joints will open and rain oil into the rain.

When the Hurricane hits, we'll lose the oil in a broken-fire-hydrant display. The rats will run up the collapsing crystal landscapes.

I'm inside this tipi. Another man, this one named Iamso, came to see me today. He wrote me a poem. He, too, suggested I help on the pipeline.

Helena—I wanted you to have better than what I was becoming.

Karen

Last night I dreamed Daniel and I were in a ball of black space. The only structure was a maze of thin yellow walkways, only a few feet wide, suspended in the air. All around me was night, and in the distance I could see Daniel walking slowly, waving, shouting that he would be there soon. I came to a fountain of electric-blue water. A woman in a white veil stood in the electric-blue water, which was pouring over her in buckets. When she reached her hand out for mine, I took it, and she pulled me into the fountain. Standing there, I felt the water as greasy fingertips spider-walking my skin. The woman in the white veil disappeared, and I took her spot. The veil was sucked to my face. The walkway beneath throbbed the color yellow. I could see down and through, and there was Daniel holding a massive green pipe and smashing the yellow walkway to triangles that slowly floated up. Beneath him there was a long staircase filled with sheep. When he looked up at me, the electric-blue water fell over him, and he told me to jump, a Hurricane was coming.

Daniel Fights a Hurricane

They had attached a section of pipe and begun the next. The exposed skin above Peter's handkerchief—cheeks, nose, and forehead—was dotted with sweat and grease. Iamso stood on the tree stump, wearing amber-tinted glasses and calling for the next section.

Daniel had lost the footrace against the two-second dreamer. In his heavy breathing, he thought he inhaled salt from the breeze.

The two-second dreamer in a squat, forearms on his

knees, looked up and smiled. Finally they were close. He spit between his feet and stood up.

They worked for a few hours, pounding narrowing pipes into homes with flash and spark. So near now, a layer of sweat on Daniel's hands and arms appeared—a tiny marsh with hairy grasses from salty pores. Daniel worked until he felt his bones bruise.

When he looked in the opposite direction with his magnifier pipe, the pipeline grew wider and wider, winding into the thirsty and terrified town. In the other direction, the ocean.

Then more steps, more pipes, the makeshift family of Daniel, Peter, Iamso, and the two-second dreamer working as a machine.

They eased into a rhythm, focused on pipes and bolts. Daniel asked Iamso to move the tree stump, Peter for another pipe, the two-second dreamer to install the tree-branch braces for each section.

Faster. Faster. Faster.

They worked through a curtain of trees.

Faster.

They finally stood on sand.

The line sloped down toward the water. Another paper boat appeared in a palmful of water. Peter unfolded it. It was from the man with tattoos, who wanted to know if they had touched water yet. He said people are so dehydrated they can't swallow their mashed potatoes. There was a brief description of a mother squeezing drops of water down a baby's mouth to lubricate the stuck mashed potatoes. Iamso responded with a quickly folded raft that read, *Yes, we are at the ocean. Expect water soon.*

Down the beach and into the ocean the pipeline went. The group rolled up their pants to slightly above their knees. Seaweed and ocean foam stuck to their calves as they entered.

At the horizon—sea and sky in matching hues of blue.

They fed the last section underwater. The waves made the process difficult, but Daniel and Iamso steadied the line. Iamso asked if the Hurricane knew they were taking water from its ocean. Daniel said the ocean doesn't belong to the Hurricane, that it's the other way around.

A long tube was inserted into the last pipe. Peter placed the other end of the tube between his lips. The waves grew to their waists, and they fought to keep their feet grounded. Peter inhaled. He moved the tube from his mouth and vomited ocean. Quickly, he dunked the tube into the water. Then they felt the pipeline shake with water.

It's working, said Iamso, trying to stay above the waves that were at their chests.

Up on the beach, the two-second dreamer was lying down. Iamso yelled for him to wake up and inspect the pipeline for leaks.

Water was coming to the town in the shape of a steel-enclosed river.

The waves went for their throats.

Peter was pulled under. When he came up, his handkerchief had slipped off and his mouth was full of bloody foam. He swam, then ran from the ocean, back up the beach, screaming from the salt filling the holes in his gums. The two-second dreamer woke, yawned a mouthful of sky that filled with rain clouds.

The horizon rose into the sky. Daniel used the pipeline like a rope to get back to shore. The wind turned their untucked shirts into rippling flags as they ran.

Clouds heavy with rain gave up and collapsed on the beach.

The pipeline swayed, creaked.

Waves leaped into the air and formed water-windowed towers.

A school of fish fell into the sky.

They ran. The water reached for the heels of their boots.

Through the forest they went, surrounded by deer, birds of a dozen different colors, squirrels, a creature covered in hair, all guided by the pipeline back into town.

Peter carried Iamso like a baby, cradling his head and telling him it would be okay.

The two-second dreamer outraced everyone and disappeared into the trees ahead.

More clouds fell into the trees, where they ripped into broken webs saturated with black rain.

The distortion fuzz of rushing water.

The Hurricane screamed ocean.

The Hurricane placed a hand on the wind and pushed, and the wind placed a hand on their backs and shoved.

Tree limbs cracked and trees fell into the water that now carried them away.

The ocean swept through the forest, the corn-husk

field, the town, and ate them whole. Daniel somersaulted underwater. Iamso tried to write something in his book as the water took him under. An owl slammed into Daniel's hip.

Daniel cut the skin of the ocean and entered air. He gasped and saw everything in swirling gray and black. The Hurricane had broken the sky in odd angles—there was an indented and crumpled area of sky that leaked a small waterfall. Trees, feathers, leaves, the collected antiques of a modest estate, the man with tattoos showing his new tattoo to the Hurricane—all flew over Daniel like thrown rice and splashed into the ocean.

Someone pulled on Daniel's ankle, and he was back underwater. It was Iamso, who waved his hands and pointed wildly to an area of dark water.

Iamso swam. Daniel followed.

Daniel tried to ask where they were going, but it sounded like GARRRRLLLAAGGBAGGGGOOOOO.

For a moment the water went clear. He saw the first large pipes connected. Then it went cloudy, his eyes filled with salt water, seaweed wrapped around his throat, fish swam up his shirtsleeves.

Iamso said back to Daniel, GARRRRRLLLLAGG-BAGGOOOOO.

Daniel thought that if the two-second dreamer drowns, enters a coma, he will have an endless chain of never-ending two-second dreams and people would never hear them whispered in their ears.

Daniel kicked with everything he had. He couldn't see. Everything was dark. He kept a hand on Iamso's leg.

He bumped his head against something hard and

cracked his foot against something harder. He yelled. Made bubbles.

Then his back was curled against a solid structure. Water flowed past. The Hurricane bashed its fists against the sky, and the ocean shifted.

Daniel closed his eyes and reran the two-second dream for his wife, Helena. He chewed ocean water as he repeated the first poem Iamso had given him.

He tried to remember what sitting in a tree felt like.

Everyone Needs a Two-Second Dream

Daniel has another visitor at his tipi—a man calling himself a two-second dreamer.

What does that mean, says Daniel, who is wringing out a shirt soaked with stream water.

I give two-second dreams for people who need them. Do you need one.

I'm not sure, says Daniel. I'm doing pretty well on my own. What are you doing out here anyway, besides giving two-second dreams.

I'm working on a pipeline that will connect to the ocean.

Daniel stabs the embers of last night's fire with a stick. The forest is green and quiet.

Bad idea, he says, hanging the shirt over a tree branch. A Hurricane is about to hit. It will destroy the pipeline and flood the entire town.

The two-second dreamer says he hopes that doesn't happen and asks if Daniel wants to help.

Why would I want to help if I think everything will be destroyed.

Daniel continues wringing out shirts. When he looks up for the two-second dreamer, he can't find him. Daniel shouts hello, but no one answers.

Later that day he decides to walk back to his car. He doesn't expect it to be there, certain it's been towed away or stolen, but it's there—covered in bird shit, leaves, a fresh dent.

He opens the door, grabs his cell phone, and turns it on. There's one blinking bar left. He calls Karen Suppleton. "It's me."

"Is this Daniel?"

"I'm Daniel. Right here. The guy who is scared of a Hurricane."

"Daniel, are you okay? Please tell me you are okay. I haven't heard from you in a while. Someone, a friend of yours, called here asking for you. Is everything okay? Daniel, I need to know, where are you right now? Tell me where you are right now."

"I'm still on vacation, but listen, I've been seeing things."

"Like?"

"People," says Daniel. He begins walking toward the woods again. "Workers from the pipeline have somehow made it out here, asking for me to come back to work. But I don't want to go back to work."

"You need to come back," says Karen Suppleton. "Where are you right now?"

"The woods. Are you eating McDonald's right now?"

Daniel hears Karen Suppleton say something to

someone else, her voice muffled from a hand over the receiver.

"Has my wife called?" he asks. "Is she worried about me?"

"What was that, Daniel? Listen, I'll pick you up. Let me know where you are. Please."

"I said I was in the woods," he tells her. "Really, I'm okay. I was just wondering how these workers got out here. The Hurricane will hit very soon."

"No one from the pipeline is with you, Daniel," says Karen Suppleton. "Daniel, I need you to stop playing around and just tell me right now where you are."

"I'm not, I know I'm not."

"What?"

"I'm okay, I think, because I have good teeth."

Village of Underwater Pipes

Daniel wakes up inside a tunnel, hears voices. There's a campfire in the narrow distance, water dripping from the ceiling and onto flames.

A group of men and women walk up the sides of the tunnel and around in a full circle. A small stream runs down the center of the tunnel, and small fish flop in the stream.

Daniel walks to an intersection of tunnels where blacksmiths are welding the angles and corners. An older gentleman with a cane in one hand holds a lantern in the other for the blacksmiths to see by. He sits atop a ladder dripping water from each rung.

Need something, he says to Daniel.

My friends, says Daniel.

Don't talk so loud, says a girl wearing black earmuffs, sitting on a lower rung of the ladder. Daniel says he's sorry, even though he's not sure for what, because he wasn't speaking that loud.

Shhhhhhh. What did I just tell you.

Where are we, he asks.

Inside a pipe.

A pipe.

Yes, a pipe. Thank goodness for that.

Later, after walking through the tunnels, Daniel finds Iamso. He tells Daniel they are now living underwater in the pipes.

What about the Hurricane, asks Daniel.

What about it, says Iamso.

Daniel taps the shoulder of a passing woman with the face of a moose. He asks where the Hurricane is. She says the Hurricane is outside the pipe walls, above the water, pacing the horizon as usual. Then she excuses herself and says she wants to try to go for a swim.

What's happening, says Daniel.

There's talk of a rubber door, says Iamso. It's like a curtain. You can leave and swim to another set of pipes. I haven't seen it yet. I bet there are jellyfish out there.

But what's happening, says Daniel.

After the moose-faced woman, Daniel stops the next person, a woman with Hurricane-sad eyes, fair skin, and a sharp chin. He asks the same question, and she replies that the Hurricane is a group of children.

What, he says.

It's children, she says. The future. Children are responsible for where we are now.

Daniel thinks, I am underwater and inside the first set of giant pipes. I am inside a village of underwater pipes, and the Hurricane is somewhere, possibly here.

The woman with the Hurricane-sad eyes pulls her hair into a side ponytail and wrings out a bucket of seawater. She says she needs dinner and the boat needs more work. She walks away and sings:

> *All canoes are filled with rain,*
> *Livin' underwater isn't the same.*
> *Yes, you, Lord,*
> *You saved me from*
> *My canoe filled with rain.*
> *Garrrr-lllaaaa-gooooo*
> *Is all you hear me sayin'*
> *When I'm underwater*
> *And not prayin'.*
> *Give me back-ack-ack*
> *My canoe filled with rain.*

Karen

I remember when we were driving to my parents' house and it started raining. It was the type of rain that came down so hard, so fast, that even the wipers couldn't keep the layers of water from the windshield. I pulled the car over with the dozens of others, a line of red lights flashing up the interstate. Daniel said weather was so terrifying because it was so unpredictable and that most people were arrogant toward it. I said it was only rain, and he said but what if it were multiplied by a thousand. We sat in the car, rain pummeling metal. Threads of lightning quilted a distant gray bridge. Daniel said something about the sky being so large and capable of terrible things. We sat in the car for twenty minutes until the rain let up, cars pulling back onto the road.

Drown

Those workers haven't come back, and I'm worried about them. Last night, while I was huddled inside my tipi, the rain fell in hard angles, the sky buzzed, and I felt the tipi rattle, as if someone had gripped the top and given it a shake.

I thought about my wife, Helena.

I sketched three predictions of my death and settled on an image of drowning in the ocean, surrounded by a floating town. I expanded the image to include the Hurricane howling above, sweeping its hands back and forth against the ocean, claws dragging through the top few inches of water.

Inside my tipi, tucked into a ball, rocking from side to side and whispering for it all to stop, I told myself I could control my thoughts.

In the morning the sky was clear and the ground wasn't wet. I spent the day gathering firewood, writing in my notebook, and when leaves blew from branches or animals knocked over rocks, I looked for the workers but saw only forest.

Karen

I kept a journal of how much Daniel spoke. He didn't believe me that he was shutting down, becoming more distant in our relationship. An example of the journal went like this:

Monday: Approx. 300 words spoken.

Tuesday: Approx. 250 words spoken.

Wednesday: Approx. 200 words spoken (left house for two hours).

Thursday: Approx. 300 words spoken (weather talk).

Friday: Approx 100 words spoken (nothing said before bed).

Saturday: Approx 75 words.

Sunday: Approx 20 words (left house for three hours).

Then there were days when Daniel didn't speak at all. A vertical line of zeros written. If I confronted him about it, said it wasn't fair to me, he would either go into the bedroom or leave for hours. Sometimes he'd take out his book with his drawings and add to it. I never showed him the journal.

I thought many times that I had made a mistake being with Daniel. But then he'd have days where he spoke thousands of words. He was such a kind person. Days of cooking dinner together and going to bed simultaneously. He'd come home from work with a big box and when I asked what was in the box, he'd smile and pull out one of twelve bottles of carbonated water. Also inside: chocolate bars, popcorn, the cat food I forgot the day before.

Daniel Walks Through the Village of Underwater Pipes

Along the pipes, lanterns were strung above. People splashed water at each other from the small stream. Their hair was wet as seaweed. The Hurricane slept around us, churned the water, moved the village of underwater pipes wherever it wanted. A few people sitting against the wall of the pipe held their ears, shook their heads no.

I followed Iamso. Many of the townsfolk wore earmuffs the color of coal and black dresses. They spoke by hand movements and ignored the screams of the Hurricane outside the pipe walls. They drank a yellowish liquid through the clear plastic tube from the last pipe that now ran from their mouths to a communal clay pot.

We walked and lost our balance—the village of underwater pipes seesaw-floating through the ocean, the stream and its fish coating the walls before dripping back into place.

Monkeys, foxes, bears, sloths, owls, raccoons, a tiger, an ape impaled with a sharp piece of coral that no one dared try to remove from his shoulder, and an elephant stuck at the end of one pipe, forming a kind of door, were all living with us inside the pipes. It smelled like rain-beaten trees, turpentine, and wet hair.

We ate fish and filtered the salt water though the clay pot and tube. Campfires were scattered throughout the village of underwater pipes. Someone strung a clothing line. Shirts and dresses attempted to dry without wind.

A part of myself fell in love with this place. It was the simple and strange idea that I could live here and any survivors were here with me.

Another part of me was scared and wanted to know how long we could stay like this. Would we need to escape. Would we run out of air. Was I, right now, killing myself by breathing too much.

Have you seen Peter or the two-second dreamer, I asked. And what about the man with tattoos—is he here.

No, I haven't seen them yet, said Iamso.

We walked from one section to the next, through welded intersections of giant pipes. How many large pipes were there. Seven, eight. I couldn't remember. How many extended from the concrete building.

Can we really live down here, I asked.

I don't see why not. Maybe it's better this way.

Iamso reached into his coat pocket and handed me a picture.

This is what it looks like if you're a whale looking at us, he said.

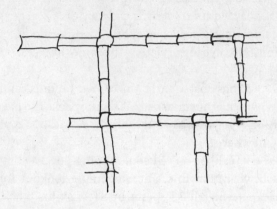

I'll show you something amazing, said Iamso.

My feet splashed through water and into steel, the bolts hitting the balls of my feet, as we ran through the village of underwater pipes lit by strung lanterns and campfires.

Exit

Today Daniel walks three and a half hours, out of the forest, and on to a country road he walks for another hour. He's done this before, for food. There's a Mobile Mart located in what can only feel like a desert.

"The young man back again, looking a little rough around the edges this time," says the owner—an elderly man wearing jeans and a white T-shirt that reads, in black cursive letters, *I ♥ NO TERRORIST*.

Daniel purchases a bag of bread, some apples, crackers, and a massive jug of water—the same things he bought weeks ago.

Daniel has lost nearly thirty-five pounds, and the owner, who has never asked his name, packs the bag.

"Slim Jim, you okay out there?"

"Out where?"

"You look like you've been camping."

"Oh, yeah, I'm fine. Just keeping a lookout for the Hurricane, which has kept me up a few nights."

"You see what happened here," says the owner.

On the front page of today's paper, there's an article with the headline OIL LEAK IN PIPELINE CAUSES DELAY, COSTS LIVES.

"Thing opened up like a pretty mouth," says the owner. "Puked oil all over the earth. You believe that?"

Daniel forces a smile, sees a creased, depleted McDonald's bag sitting on a shelf behind the owner, says thank you, and, trying not to collapse in tremors before he gets to the door, walks straight back to his tipi in the forest with his bag of goods.

Karen

I'm waiting for Daniel to call again. I'm waiting and thinking I should call the police. I've been taking long walks and thinking, *Daniel is a grown man he can take care of himself you have your own life to live,* followed by, *He can't take care of himself, you are still part of his life.* I go to the movies alone and don't think about Daniel because I give myself over to the world of the movie. I remember Daniel and me going to the movies, and at random times he'd squeeze my leg, just above the knee.

Lantern Light

The first thought I have when I wake up inside the village of underwater pipes is of a small pile of burning feathers. And inside that pile of burning feathers is the thought that if my wife was missing, and survived, she was here with me. She would be singing and building ladders from salt-encrusted pipes to hang paper sculptures. A hobby she loves very much.

It's nice to meet everyone, I say to the group Iamso has introduced me to.

The women sit in a row against a curve of pipe, stitching quilts, and the one man, the only man, builds a boat from scraps of broken homes several feet away. They refer to themselves as deserts, and when I ask where the name comes from, they explain that if anything can swallow a Hurricane, it's a desert.

Listen to their plan, says Iamso. It's really something. He takes out a book and writes.

It's more of an idea, says one of the women.

It's pretty good, says another. Not perfect, but it's going to make things happen that need to happen, if you know what I mean.

Spots of lantern light shift with the swaying of the village, illuminating the man building the boat, then the women stitching the quilt.

Tell him, says Iamso. What the plan, what the idea is.

A woman pulls a red thread up and almost to the lantern before placing her needle on her lap. Once he finishes the boat, she says, we'll leave the village of underwater pipes, swim to the top, and, from the boat, attack the Hurricane.

72 | Iamso smiles and writes so fast he's about to tear through the page.

So you think you'll be able to see the Hurricane, I ask.

Of course, she says.

The women stand up and stretch the quilt out to admire their progress. It's a sail, the word DESERTS crudely stitched along an edge.

I try to imagine everyone fitting into such a small boat, rolling over the waves of the ocean, hurling pipes at the pale face of the Hurricane.

Terrible children, says one of the women.

Iamso looks at me, shrugs his shoulders, and goes back to writing.

Terrible children, I ask.

The Hurricane, says another woman. The Hurricane

is a group of children. They brought the flood, and the wind, and the yanking of nails from our homes.

So they live somewhere on the ocean, asks Iamso.

One of the women elbows the one sitting next to her. Yes, she says. They live in their own boat, or on an island—how am I supposed to know exactly.

And we'll kill them, says another, looking embarrassed for the outburst. I mean, we're going to take care of it.

Someone mumbles something about a bag of blow darts, to make sure the bag is full. The man stops sanding the boat, looks up, sighs, then goes back to sanding, shaking his head as the lantern light sways and he enters a moment of pipe-living darkness. I thought I saw a tattoo on his arm but couldn't tell for sure, and when the lantern light came back to him, his sleeves were rolled down and the boat was finished.

We should go, says Iamso.

Iamso holds up his book. The page reads, *We should go if we want to survive.* Also, *It will be fun. An adventure.*

I write on the same page, *I'm not sure,* and Iamso writes back, *What if we run out of air,* and I think for a while, see the women filling up bags labeled with different weapons, and write back, *Okay let me think about it.*

As the women and the man prepare the boat, they explain that they don't believe in Hurricane as weather. I say the Hurricane looked like a flash of wind and water, lightning spiderwebbing a black sky, a flood that swallowed our town and continues to haunt.

That doesn't make any sense, one of the women says.

The Hurricane is ten children wearing black dresses. They wear black earmuffs as well. For what reason, we don't know.

One or two may be living here with us, says another one of the women, who watches the man organizing the bags in the boat. We're not sure, but it's possible.

The children, whatever they are, as Hurricane, brought the ocean into our town, says another, rolling up the quilted sail.

We agree to leave tomorrow morning, which none of us will recognize living down here, so we settle on four hours of sleep. Iamso tells me we'll get help and rescue the village of underwater pipes, that it's the only way.

Before we disband for dinner followed by sleep, everyone practices sitting in the boat. All of us, knees pulled to chests, squeeze to fit.

At night Iamso and I sleep in a section of the village of underwater pipes known as Bird's Nest. Tree branches, twigs, leaves, feathers, and string are shaped into beds and chairs. It smells like mud, smoke, wet clothing.

I stay up listening to the whispered echoes of the deserts finalizing their plan. Again they ask the man if he's brought enough weapons, and I don't hear his reply. Fish flop in the stream. The village of underwater pipes floats through the sea. I imagine our broken homes, shredded streets, the pulled-out hair of grassy fields, our town's black destruction that didn't make it here, all of it a cruel clump of sea life outside us.

Iamso slips into a rhythmic snore.

I can't sleep. The thought that in several hours we'll

be on the ocean surface, in a boat, sends me on a walk through the pipes, searching for Helena.

Maybe she's down here.

Through the pipes I go, losing my way, the village tipping to the left and my body following, hand-crawling along the wall.

I pass men and women sleeping against burlap sacks filled with the remains of houses. Two women playing the ukulele smile as I pass them, splashing their legs with stream water.

Helena, I whisper. Helena, are you here somewhere. If you are, say . . . rainwater in a canoe . . . and keep saying it until I find you.

I walk the entire village of underwater pipes. I get lost, try to retrace my steps, trip over a burned-out campfire, bump my head against a string of lanterns, and say hello to a woman who isn't Helena building a ladder from pipes encrusted with salt.

The Hurricane places its face into the ocean and blows bubbles. I clutch my ears, fall to my knees that bruise on the steel pipe, and get soaked with water. Teeth clenched, hands on the floor, I feel the coolness, then the warmth, of the buzzing ocean.

I follow the sound of ukuleles and work my way back through the sleeping village of underwater pipes, campfires dying, people mumbling in their Hurricane nightmares, birds trying to fly and looking like bats. I turn a corner that leaks ocean water. Then I'm at a place where lanterns and paper shapes are hung. Boats, canoes, fish, all folded paper hanging by string from a pipe ceiling.

One at a time, I take each down and unfold.

Come and find me—Sarah.

                              I am so thirsty—Thomas

    Hold your breath—Melli

                We will drown here—Olla

    My socks are wet—George

                    Someone please help me—Anne

We might die in here—(Blank)

I open hundreds until I unfold an octopus that reads, *Everything will be okay—Helena*

Back at Bird's Nest, I try to wake Iamso and tell him about the octopus note. He slaps my hand away, eyes closed, mumbles nightmares about the Hurricane. Go away, he says. Just go away, you . . . Don't bother us anymore, you.

A Short History of Daniel

Daniel decides to move his campsite deeper into the forest. He exits one forest, walks through a wide cornhusk field, and enters another. There's an opening, an area with grass and trees. He sets up his tipi under a large tree with lots of shade and spends the afternoon walking around the grassy area, surveying the sky.

When Daniel was a child, he disappeared on multiple occasions. Each time he said it was because he needed to get away from the Hurricane.

The first disappearance happened when he was eleven. He was found in the forest after three days, and his excuse was that a group of men had told him to come there, that a Hurricane was approaching. He described the three men in such vivid detail that the police sketched three faces and set a cash reward. No one was found, but one man with horrible teeth was questioned extensively.

The second disappearance came a year later. This time Daniel went missing for three hours, at night, shortly after bedtime. His parents found him in the backyard digging a hole in the dark. When they asked him what he was doing, he said the pipeline workers were knocking on the ceiling to the backyard because they were trying to run away from the Hurricane. He described a flood of ocean and oil and how they would live underwater in the giant pipes. For six months his parents sent him to a child psychologist before giving up and telling their friends and family that Daniel *just has a very active imagination.*

The third disappearance came two years after the second, when Daniel locked himself inside a McDonald's bathroom. The police were called. They remembered Daniel from his first disappearance and asked in a mocking tone if it was the Hurricane.

"The Hurricane," Daniel said with tears in his eyes, being escorted out of the McDonald's. "I closed the door there, and it locked, and I couldn't open it. That's happened before. Why do doors lock behind me? Why am I like this?"

"A tiger climbed a tree," Daniel, age eight, said to his mother.

"A squirrel?"

"No, a tiger. It had stripes and was big. It ran up the tree because the forest floor was filling with water."

"You have some imagination," said his mother.

"It's not my imagination, though. It's real. I saw it."

Later, in his twenties, Daniel stopped running away and hiding and began having panic attacks. In his convulsions he'd create entire new worlds. He followed in his father's footsteps and got a job working on the pipeline. The distraction of work, of becoming obsessed with pipes, appeared to help. Over the years the panic attacks seemed to spread out, but the visions were still there: new people, new work, his wife becoming more unrecognizable when he came home from work, his wife feeling the distance between them, wanting to help and not knowing how. Daniel alone: talking to someone in the bathroom.

List of Deserts Who Live in the Village of Underwater Pipes

A group of five people originally hid from the Hurricane in the home of a woman named Ruth. When the Hurricane hit, they were pulled into the ocean and found safety inside the pipes. They have quickly become friends and staunch enemies of the Hurricane.

The five people include four women and one man:

Isabella (age fifty-nine): Born during a lightning storm that cut all power to the birthing room. Most of her childhood spent hiding, stitching quilts and sewing flags in the comfort of dark closets. Short, pale skin, curly hair the color of milk and sand.

Kimberly (age sixty-seven): Born during an earthquake. Most of her childhood spent jumping on a bed and adulthood asking strange men to shake her. Tall, pale skin, thinning gray hair.

Mary (age forty-two): Born on the beach. Most of her childhood spent swimming in the ocean. Enjoyed staying underwater until near drowning, but then would end up gasping for air while crawling up the sand, crying and asking for help. Short, chubby, wears a hat made from corn husks.

Ruth (age seventy-eight): Born during a windstorm that blew her laboring mother through a window and down the street. Childhood spent flying paper birds and trying to understand wind and the wet feel of it on her skin. Tall, balding, wears men's boots.

Oliver (age thirty-eight): Son of Kimberly. Born during a shaking ceremony conducted by a strange man. Remembers very little of his childhood. Looks familiar to Daniel. Wears long sleeves.

Karen

At the grocery store, I run into my neighbor Allison again. She asks if I'm okay, says that I look like I've lost weight, and *she doesn't mean to insult me, but* I have dark circles under my eyes. I tell her Daniel hasn't called or shown up at my house for weeks and weeks, and I'm worried, but I don't know what to do. I have no idea where he is. What would I even tell the police? I imagine a search party of thousands and being interviewed by the local news.

"You need to call," says Allison. "This isn't just someone missing, this is someone who needs help."

"I know," I say. "I know, I know, I'm an awful person."

"You're not an awful person."

Later that night I sit on the couch with my laptop and click on photos of me and Daniel. My favorite is the one of us at the lake. The sky is filled with clouds, and it's just about ready to rain, but Daniel is standing in four inches of water, and I'm there, and he's holding me, and we're both smiling as boats pass in the distance.

He's okay, I tell myself. *He's an adult with his own life, and it's not my responsibility to take care of someone else.*

It's raining again.

80 |

Door

At the new campsite in the woods Daniel thinks there's a door in the grass. Yes, he was meant to come here. Yes, in some twisted way it will all make sense as time continues. *Yes,* he thinks, *everything will be okay*, and lies down on the grassy door and falls asleep.

Hum

Daniel woke to Iamso frying fish skin in a pan he held over a small pile of burning feathers. The ukulele players ran by in loud metal splashes, chased by the ape with the coral stuck in his shoulder. Daniel thought, Maybe they tried to soothe him with a song before trying to pull the coral out.

He took a bite of fish. The Hurricane's fists pounded the ocean. A loud *thump* pushed Daniel's head deep between his shoulders. He looked up, paused midbite, until it passed.

Daniel asked if Iamso could tell him how he was currently feeling. Iamso said he wrote something earlier and showed him a page in his book.

I know it's not very good, said Iamso, taking back the book. I like my others much better.

Someone rang a bell. The walls of the village of underwater pipes vibrated in a gentle hum. Daniel and Iamso finished their fish skin and straightened their Bird's Nest beds before walking toward the sound.

The sound took them to the deserts: Isabella, Kimberly, Mary, and Ruth. They were ready to leave. Oliver, the son of Kimberly, smashed a bell on a two-inch string with a blue pipe, hesitant and careful not to hit his fingers.

In the Woods Daniel Sees the Hurricane as Monster

I see the Hurricane as a monster who walks on water and bumps his head on the sky. He stops and unhinges his jaw. Underwater villagers put ladders up to his mouth. They climb up with burlap bags of salt slung over their shoulders and empty the knife-cut bags onto his tongue. When he's had enough, the Hurricane walks again. The ladders fall away, and the villagers dive, splash, into the ocean. Clouds of salt dust fill the air that the Hurricane runs to gobble up, his feet smashing against the ocean in steel-drum echoes.

Tonight I see the Hurricane as I've never seen it before. I hope this square in the grass is a door. The sky tastes like salt.

Leaving the Village of Underwater Pipes

The plan created by the deserts:

1. Leave the village of underwater pipes where the stuck elephant is.
2. Once near the stuck elephant, the welders will construct a wall behind us and seal us in. We'll then be standing between the new wall and the elephant.
3. Push the elephant out of the pipe and let the rush of ocean water carry us and the boat to the surface.

4. At the surface find the boat, get in, and seek out the Hurricane.
5. Confront the Hurricane.
6. Find a way to rescue the village of underwater pipes.

Oliver drags the boat by a thick rope. Everyone in the village of underwater pipes follows Oliver and the deserts, their expressions rain-destructed and Hurricane-sad-eyed. Some carry lanterns. Some pray for their safety. The sound of two ukuleles fills the pipes. People start to cheer, DEFEAT THE HURRICANE! Someone throws confetti made of sawdust.

When they reach the end of the pipe and the sleeping-stuck elephant, the crowd stays back. The welders begin working on the wall to seal them off. They lift huge sheets of scrap metal created from pounded-out and welded pipes, lower their glasses, and the sparks pour into the stream.

The elephant's back is in the ocean. His four feet are scrunched together in a box near his face, which is dirty from underwater-pipe living. The deserts walk up close and hold their lanterns against his feet and eyes, trying to see spots of ocean in the cracks. He whistles in his sleep, the elephant. Daniel hums along and places a hand on part of his trunk.

Behind them the welders hammer the bolts to finish up. There's still a space that needs to be sealed off. The ukulele players play a parting song, and some sing: *Push me out if you want to! I'm an elephant! So what! Push me out if you want to! No one taught me how to swim! Oh, no! Push me out if you want to! I can't swim!*

Many of the animals, including the ape with the coral stuck in his shoulder, watch the group watching the elephant.

Karen

I remember when I first met Daniel. We were both hired at the same time at a bookstore. The supervisor introduced me to everyone and finally to Daniel, who was shelving books. Later, when my mom asked about the people at the new job, I said, "There's a Daniel."

I didn't last long at that job, but I continued to see Daniel. I'd pick him up from work, and we'd drive to Red Ridge Mountain and hike to a spot overlooking the town. We'd drink cold beer I bought before picking him up. We did this for a few weeks before Daniel moved in with me.

"Don't you think that's a little fast?" my mom asked.

"Yes. It is fast," I said.

With Daniel everything felt fun and fast at first.

Banana Bomb

Another hour, the wall is almost finished. A small good-bye door, the size of a mailbox, is the last opening to be sealed off. Through the opening, Daniel hears a loud

Shhhhhhhhhh and then *Everyone please be quiet, we don't want to wake the elephant.* A slight breeze moves through the good-bye door, and Daniel feels it through his damp hair. Good-bye, everyone whispers through the good-bye door before the welders cover it with a square of metal. We hope to see you again.

Kimberly asks Daniel if he's found his wife yet.

Not yet, he says. I looked last night but couldn't find her.

Oliver is about to say something when Ruth raises a finger to his lips. The Hurricane probably has her, she says.

Isabella pets the elephant's curled-up trunk, turns and smiles at Daniel. We'll get her back, she says.

Iamso asks if there's a plan yet to rescue the village of underwater pipes.

Not yet, says Mary. First things first, defeat the Hurricane. | *85*

And get your wife back, says Ruth.

We're family now, says Mary.

Iamso pounds his fist on the good-bye door and screams, We are leaving now.

Someone yells back a muffled Be careful and come back soon.

Daniel, Iamso, and the deserts place their backs against the elephant, dig their heels into the muddy and wet floor of the pipe, and push.

The elephant whistles louder. His body moves out an inch or two, some water sprays between two feet, and the ocean shoves him back into the pipe.

Get ready, the deserts say. It's going to happen quickly. Prepare your ears and lungs for ocean.

Each of the deserts has a bag marked with a symbol for the weapon inside:

= pipe

= knife

= blow dart

= rope

= banana bomb

What's a banana bomb, asks Daniel, who with the rest of the group leans back and pushes again against the elephant.

Kimberly lets out a loud grunt. It's basically a bunch of rotten bananas, she says. Believe me, it's painful when you get rotten banana in your eyes and open sores. Very effective.

Why would someone have open sores, asks Daniel.

You throw them like a grenade, and when they hit, they splatter everywhere, you see, they explode, she says. Her face clenches, and she throws her shoulders back into the elephant.

Someone shouts at Oliver to push harder, he's not trying hard enough. Oliver says in a defeated tone that he's doing the best he can. He stops for a moment to roll up his sleeves. The deserts all yell, Come on now.

On Oliver's forearm a tattoo reads, *HURRICANE* ♥ *YOU*.

Then more shouting. Ruth calls for a three count. She says they not only need Oliver to push more but they need a powerful cohesive force.

One.

Two.

Three.

Push.

And nothing.

When the elephant refuses to budge against the pressure of the ocean, Ruth says everyone is weak. Daniel imagines her holding a whip.

Oliver stands next to Daniel and whispers, Good to see you again.

So it is you, he says.

Another count to three.

One.

Two.

Three.

Push.

This time the elephant moves, water sprays from the holes around his body, his unfolding trunk and extending legs slip from the ass of the pipe, and a flood of ocean pours into the pipe, rolls everyone up the new welded wall. The town yells, Be careful, to the furious strumming of double ukuleles. And out they go, pulled into the ocean.

Karen

There was an evening when I came home from work and all the lights were off. Daniel was in the bedroom with the curtains drawn. He was lying under a single sheet and had it stretched like a tent by using his knees and hands. When I asked him what he was doing, he said he was being safe.

"Can I come in?" I asked.

"Of course."

I climbed under the sheet and helped make the tent even larger. I sat and expanded the tent toward the ceiling.

"See," he said. "Doesn't it feel safe here?"

"It does. It's fun. Your face looks funny."

"It's the light. Your face looks like a mask."

I kissed Daniel and let the tent collapse over us.

"Oh, no," said Daniel.

I pushed myself up a few inches from Daniel's face. "What? What's wrong?"

"Nothing. Feels even safer now."

A Series of Quick, Sharp Waves

The water is clear, and Daniel sees the elephant somersaulting ahead of him. Oliver floats past with the boat tethered to his wrist. The elephant is awake, eyes open, feet running, trunk stretched skyward as a school of fish surround him.

When Isabella, Mary, Ruth, and Kimberly are spit from the end of the pipe, their bodies appear bomb-exploded, wrists strung by rope carrying weapon bags, waists tied with rope chaining them together as they try to gain control of their arms and legs in the thick rush and spin of the sea.

Iamso swims near Daniel and points up to a lighter shade of ocean where the sky might be. Below Daniel, the village of underwater pipes as Iamso had drawn it, looking smaller and smaller.

Daniel is the first to taste air.

The deserts follow in gasps.

Ruth gasps so loudly that Daniel thinks a cloud could be sucked into her mouth. Isabella pops up with a yelp. Kimberly and Oliver hold each other and slap their arms in the small waves of the ocean. Mary shivers with big blue lips.

Kimberly and Oliver separate, and the boat spikes up between them.

Daniel thinks he sees land in the distance, says so aloud, then realizes it's only the elephant's body.

Sorry, he says, treading water, spitting water.

Everyone swims to the boat.

The sky carries a handful of clouds in a blue net. The water is calm, with little tents of waves. Daniel looks for the Hurricane.

Iamso is the first to climb in, the rest of the group steadying the boat and then following.

Ruth puts up the quilted sail, which is heavy with water. She says it will take only one good Hurricane-style breeze to dry and move them along. If not, there's a motor attached to the back of the boat.

Oliver is the last person to get in. The other deserts yell at him to hurry up.

The sail dries from a warm breeze but doesn't carry the boat. Someone says they need to hurry. Oliver yanks the cord on the rusty motor, and it starts with a pop.

The boat's nose points at the sun as they propel forward, all of them hugging their knees to make room, eyes narrow from the wind, the boat bouncing over the choppy waves, the blue sky following.

Oliver steers the wooden handle of the motor. The other deserts check their weapon bags and squeeze the sleeves of their dresses dry. Their wet hair and the bouncing of the boat creates a mist on Daniel's face as they travel. Iamso's writing again. He doesn't seem to care about the drops of water bubbling the thin pages of his book.

Could get foggy, says Oliver.

Do you ever shut up, says Ruth.

I never talk, Oliver says. I haven't said more than a sentence today.

They ride around the ocean looking for the Hurricane until the horizon goes crooked with mountains.

The boat jumps a large wave and lands with a slap. On impact Daniel sees a flash, an image, of a tipi darted with rain. Ruth almost falls out. Mary grabs her by the shoulders and pulls her back in. The sun blinks yellow and folds into itself, goes dull. Dark clouds crowd. A puddle falls from the sky and soaks Kimberly, whose hair has just dried.

A heavy rain begins, and the deserts scream for the

Hurricane to show itself. Daniel sees himself in the tipi. People around him are yelling.

Isabella rubs circles on Daniel's back and says, There, there, it will be okay.

Then a series of quick, sharp waves—*whackwhack-whack*—before the salty air falls away under a blanket of fog.

See, says Oliver. Fog.

Mary takes a pipe from the bag and throws it at the sky in no clear direction. It pinwheels through the sky before being swallowed by the fog and the shadow of a mountain.

Daniel asks what she threw the pipe at, and Mary shrugs, throws another, yells.

Ruth grips a cheese knife in each hand, holding them low in the hull of the boat.

The fog clears, just enough to see, and they slide up a beach.

Oliver steps from the boat and pulls it onto the sand.

Daniel stands up in the boat, sees a large bridge that extends from the center of the landmass and out over the water and into another fog.

Mary throws another pipe. This one spirals into a grassy field beyond the sand and rocks. It lands with a dull thud. Isabella tells her to stop.

Each of the deserts pulls her own dress from a weapon bag, Oliver a pair of brown pants and a blue button-down shirt. They wring everything out.

Fog hugs cables on the bridge before it's sliced into a white fade.

The sky pops blue and cloudless, and the sound forces Daniel to shut his eyes in fear.

Horses eat in the grassy field. And beyond them a group of children dressed in black, wearing earmuffs, standing still in a straight line, pointing at Daniel.

Daniel in the Woods

My tipi and campsite are set up in this field between two forests. I'm starving. I'm waiting. The sky pops blue and cloudless, and the sound is deafening. I saw a boat and more. Somewhere a pipeline of oil is breathing into the floor of the ocean.

Karen

I call more friends, and they all agree to contact the police, and they all say they will volunteer to look for Daniel. They say the police can probably track his cell phone, and from there people can scan the woods. They all tell me Daniel will be okay.

After Daniel left for good, the end of our marriage, Daniel completely gone from what I called the real world, which he always laughed at, the single hardest thing was sleeping alone. The subtraction of a body in bed. Gentle breathing, even snoring, replaced with silence. Daniel has a tenderness about him, and when I couldn't sleep, he'd do this thing where he would slip his hand under my shirt and rub my back in circles until I fell asleep. He waited for me to be asleep before he slept.

Hurricane as Children

That's the Hurricane, said Mary, pointing back at the children.

Can they see us, asked Kimberly. I bet they can if we can see them.

This should do the trick, said Ruth, grabbing a banana bomb from the bag appropriately labeled.

Oliver was still in the water, pulling the boat higher up and onto the sand. Iamso hugged my leg. Ruth hurled the bananas in a rotten-brown arc, over the horses, and into what they believed was the Hurricane, these children.

Kimberly covered her eyes with the sleeve of her dress.

The children scattered, and the banana bomb became mush on the grass. A small chunk landed on a child's leg, and he fell down to pick it off.

The sky was cloudless, but there was lightning.

All the deserts held their weapons. Ruth prepared another banana bomb.

I crouched down with Iamso and watched Mary fling pipes without looking. Ruth threw another banana bomb,

Isabella dressed her rope with a noose, and Kimberly stabbed the empty air with knives.

Oliver came back from the curl of the ocean. He didn't have a weapon, so he formed fists and a scowl and looked pathetically out of place.

The fog came back in for a moment, we moved forward, and when it cleared, the children surrounded us. They showed us glances of knives and told the deserts to drop their weapons. When Ruth said she'd rather die by the hands of the Hurricane than give up, one of the children stepped forward in a stabbing manner. Ruth dropped the bananas she was holding, and everyone followed, even Oliver relaxing to open hands.

The children introduced themselves. Each stepped forward to whisper Hurricane and then stepped back.

Iamso was writing again. He asked if I'd like a poem so I could feel how I was feeling, and I said, No, it's not the time, and he said it was the perfect time because my heart was beating so fast, so much blood moving through my body.

I looked back toward the water and tried to imagine where we had come from. In the distance, at the horizon, I saw a small hump of land and nothing else.

The Hurricane apologized for the show of knives. Seven or eight years old, five boys, six girls, all with long hair. The deserts stood rigid and guarded. Kimberly and Ruth spoke loudly, a near scream, about how these children had destroyed their town, which now was underwater in a village of pipes.

We did that, one of the Hurricanes asked. The others adjusted their earmuffs.

Of course you did, said Isabella, who stood behind Ruth. Don't you—

You're the Hurricane, interrupted Mary. That's what Hurricanes do. They bring wind and rain and flooding. The sky does terrible things to itself. And that's what you did.

We're sorry about your town, one of the Hurricanes said.

A few of the children played a game of tag around the grassy field, their hair tossed up by the breeze they created. I thought I felt a drop of rain on my shoulder, but the sky was clear again.

The Hurricane, these children, these kids, walked up to each of the deserts, these old women so angry that their hands were balled up against their hips, and the children gave them each a hug, and I watched their arms soften and hug back.

We want to show you something, a Hurricane said to Ruth, who I think was crying, saying she was so sorry, her anger got the best of her. It might help explain that it's not our fault.

The boys ran to a spot on the grassy field and molded themselves around an imaginary door. They pulled the grass up by its hair, and a door opened.

Inside was a long wooden staircase the color red.

You need to run down the staircase, said a girl Hurricane. That's the only trick here. You can't stop running.

I asked what happens if you do stop. What if you get tired. Or trip and fall.

Oh, we don't know, she said. We only know there were more of us before. The others stopped running.

Karen

Tonight it rains, and I try not to imagine Daniel outside, scared. When I fall asleep on the couch, the television flashing light in the dark, I imagine him in a desert with a cloudless sky. A green stream runs the length of the desert. The dream flashes with light and dark, and in the moments of light I see Daniel leaping back and forth over the green stream. In one flash he's midstream midair, legs spread. In the next, both feet planted in the sand, a hand also on the ground for balance. The next flash: Daniel with one leg up, ready to jump back across. At the far end of the green stream, there's a giant man wearing nothing but a white veil over his face. He's hairless. His fingernails are long, with spindles of spit attached to each. With his massive hands, his body crouched, feet straddling the green stream, he sweeps sand into the water. I tell Daniel to run, and the giant looks up, and he's now holding an umbrella, and I wake up on the couch with the television flashing.

Staircase

The staircase descends into a musty dusk, and Daniel is Hurricane-scared. A banister runs on either side. Beneath the stairs tall wooden beams spiraled in vines support the structure. The Hurricane and the deserts run ahead, taking long strides over the wide, flat stairs. Iamso tells Daniel to hurry up, they stop running, and soon they're sprinting, catching up to the others, who turn and descend deeper into the winding staircase, the support beams getting shorter and thicker with vines as they approach a village below.

Daniel is careful not to step on the heels of Iamso, who runs directly in front of him. During a twist in the staircase, he looks over the banister corner and sees the deserts' heads below.

At the bottom there's a field and in the field a village.

After the last step is leaped, Mary collapses on the ground. Iamso leans on Daniel as they both try to catch their breath, slow their thumping hearts. The Hurricane stands quietly, barely breathing and smiling at the bright sight of the village.

Is this it, asks Ruth. Is this what you wanted to show us.

Daniel admires the red staircase that rises to a black cloud ceiling. He imagines an irrigation system, the best and strongest pipes running below each banister. The tallest support beam is taller than any tree he has ever seen.

This isn't only it, says one of the Hurricanes.

The Hurricane shows them the village, which is much like their village was before going underwater. Dozens of small, shacklike homes, dirt-raked streets, and a heavy crowd of people buying fruits and vegetables from vendors. Also dozens of wells and hundreds of pipes running across the roofs of homes, through the roads, around a hole in the ground, and off into the distance of black cloud.

Where do the pipes go, asks Daniel.

We've never walked far enough to find out, says one of the Hurricanes.

Never, says another.

It might go to a lake, another says.

Or a really big puddle.

A puddle so big it should be called a lake, says another.

They meet a man named Thomas. Thomas is short and pear-shaped, with muscular arms. Cleanly shaved, he has black, slicked-back hair. His eyes are dark and sunken, with no sign of eyebrows or lashes.

We have the world's greatest water system down here, says Thomas.

Daniel looks for a horizon but sees none. When he blinks, he sees himself opening a door in a grassy field. He sees himself coming up from a staircase, and he sees himself looking down at himself coming up.

It rains, says Thomas, who offers his hand to the sky, about fourteen times a week. Fresh water runs through our pipes night and day, which feeds our crops on what I consider a perfect schedule.

Daniel, the deserts, and the Hurricane look up at the raindrops, which are like globs of honey. The villagers fetch wooden buckets to collect the rainwater. Thomas remarks that if it rained more than fourteen times a week, they'd all drown.

It's really something else, says Isabella.

Is this what you wanted to show us, says Ruth. Is this it.

There's something else, says one of the Hurricanes.

We've thought about installing a moat, says Thomas.

Iamso draws in his book and hands it to Thomas.

Yes, says Thomas. Just like that.

Daniel admires how green, a burning neon, the field is. In the distance the staircase looks distorted with the black clouds, like elephants on top of stilts.

Go ahead, one of the villagers says to Daniel, placing a wooden bucket filled with rainwater next to him. Touch it.

Daniel dips his hand into the rainwater. It feels like jelly, molasses, syrup, a clear and edible honey jam.

Before you go, says Thomas, you should probably see the pipe room.

So is that it. Is that what you wanted to show us, says Ruth.

Yes.

Uh-huh.

Yup.

They walk through the village. The deserts ask the Hurricane about the clawing of clouds, the stains on the sky, the drowning of the town. The Hurricanes move their hands when they speak to show how, down here, they don't generate wind. Their earmuffs, down here, are worn around their necks.

If you're safe down here, Iamso says, then why do you even bother going back outside.

Children aren't allowed to live here, says Thomas.

The group crosses a wooden bridge that extends over a river of blue pipes. The village grows smaller behind them, with the sound of diminishing rain.

Why not, asks Daniel.

We're too unpredictable, says one of the Hurricanes, skipping alongside Daniel.

It's just easier, says Thomas.

Up ahead is a large concrete building that Thomas says houses the pipe room. A group of colored horses scatter away from it and whatever sky, whatever strange light above, turns bright.

Daniel asks Thomas if he knows a woman named Helena, perhaps lost. It's the first time he thinks maybe that's not her name. He can't remember.

Sounds familiar, says Thomas. Is she a girl, though. Maybe a Hurricane.

No, says Daniel. A woman. She's my wife.

I'm sorry, but no. I've never met a Helena over the age of, say, ten, says Thomas.

Everyone nears the large concrete building, and Daniel thinks how familiar it looks. He explains to Thomas the construction of a pipeline to the ocean for oil, then says no, water, we live by drinking water. The wells had dried up. And then the Hurricane came and flooded everything.

The deserts, says Daniel, think the Hurricane is these children here.

The Hurricane, the children, have run far up the path. They pretend to shoot the fleeing horses.

Oh, no, says Thomas. Maybe they could knock down small trees, break a window or two, flood an opium den, but that's about it.

The ocean moved, says Daniel. It moved right into our town, and the survivors, including myself and Iamso, had to live in pipes underwater. People are still down there. People are missing, like the man with tattoos and a man named Peter, who is very beautiful but has terrible teeth. We need to find them.

They stood at the door to the large concrete building. From a front pant pocket, Thomas takes out a key, unlocks the door, and pushes it open.

In we go, he says, and the Hurricane floods into the building, followed by the deserts, who look hesitant, peek their heads inside, then walk in.

Once inside, Thomas locks the door. The building is one large room filled with hundreds, if not thousands, of different-size pipes: spiderwebbed, bundled like sticks, and stuck together in rising towers. Windows looking out to black fan out across the four walls, chest level, and Daniel notices several more doors, which Thomas walks to and locks with the key.

When he comes back to Daniel, he says that on the opposite side, through all the pipes, Daniel will find a small door leading to a long pipe to shimmy through. It will take him back to the staircase. The pipe will be long and cold, but it shouldn't be a problem if Daniel just came from living underwater in a village of pipes. Really, very easy.

And take Iamso, says Thomas. I like him very much.

Daniel asks why they can't just all leave together.

I'm not sure we appreciate what the deserts stand for, says Thomas. I'm protective, in an odd sense, and from what I heard, of the attack on the beach and all . . . umm, it doesn't really sit well.

The Hurricane climbs three large pipes and takes turns sliding down, ducking beneath the smaller pipes that weave above them. The deserts watch and talk among themselves. Kimberly and Ruth are in a corner arguing. Ruth grips a knife she had hidden in her boot. Oliver takes one turn sliding down the pipe and looks embarrassed when Isabella shakes her head no, her arms crossed.

And take him as well, says Thomas, pointing at Oliver. The man with the tattoos. He's also a good one. I hope you find your wife.

The argument between Kimberly and Ruth gets louder. They're discussing whether they have forgotten why they came here in the first place—to kill the Hurricane. Ruth moves the knife back and forth in front of her chest as she yells. Everyone looks. The Hurricane stops using the pipe room like a jungle gym. Ruth, face red and bloated and old, her dress and hair still damp with the stench of ocean, shouts at them. Is this it. Is this what you wanted to show us down here finally, some room. It's all your fault, she says, sobbing. You're to blame just because you are.

The door I mentioned, says Thomas, is right over there. You'd best go.

Daniel and Iamso run to the door and wave Oliver over.

Thomas yells that the deserts shouldn't have come here wishing harm on children.

We should leave, says Daniel. We need to save the village of underwater pipes.

Did he give you any ideas, asks Iamso.

He said the ideas will come from someone else.

Should we wait for the deserts.

No, we need to leave now.

Daniel opens the door, which is more of a seal to the end of the pipe. The three take turns looking in.

If we need to go, we'll go, says Iamso, and he is the first one in, followed by Oliver.

When Daniel faces the screams, the Hurricane appears to have doubled. He blinks, and it triples. From the ends of all the pipes, in all different sizes, children pour out, filling the room. The deserts scream and run toward the locked doors. Ruth tries to stab a little girl Hurricane wearing glasses, and a dozen Hurricanes grab and twist her limbs. Ruth says they are to blame for so much destruction and someone needs to be punished. She's tired and losing her mind. They toss Ruth into the ceiling of the pipe room. Isabella and Mary try to catch her but are held back by the expanding Hurricane. Ruth's body crumples into a pile on the floor and is then trampled by hundreds of little Hurricane feet. Through the small spaces between bodies, Daniel sees Thomas exit out an open window, his legs dangling out before flipping forward and disappearing.

Daniel squeezes backward into the pipe. The room continues to fill with children, thousands of legs and tiny angry faces climbing on top of one another, their bodies on top of one another now and rising into the ceiling.

A bruised and bleeding Mary, a pipe gash on her forehead, drowns in a sea of feet.

Daniel shifts back a few inches, and a child's face bends down to him and whispers, You better hurry up. You have hero's work to do.

The last thing Daniel hears before finding his rhythmic shift through the pipe is a door clicking open.

And the Hurricane, all the children, spill out of the large concrete building through a single door that Thomas has opened. Running, laughing, jumping, and falling on top of one another, they split into smaller groups who run into the town and through streets sticky with rain.

They crawled through the tunnel, the sound of children's laughter and shouts of Hooray fading.

Daniel asked Oliver if he could call him the man with tattoos.

I like Oliver, said the man with tattoos.

Me, too, said Daniel. It's easier to say.

The three moved in a tight line of marching elbows and knees until they came to a door. Iamso pushed it open. A ladder of salt-encrusted pipes extended from the opening. They climbed down.

Did you see that, Oliver said.

I knew that would happen, said Iamso.

You knew, said Oliver, those kids, that Hurricane, was going to do that.

Pretty positive, said Iamso. And it did happen. I wrote it all down.

They stood at the bottom of a spiraling metal staircase. Daniel asked if they had to run up the stairs like they had to run down the red staircase. Iamso said running down the staircase was a joke-game by Thomas and the Hurricane, at the deserts' expense.

But they didn't want to take any chances. So they ran.

Up the staircase, ascending higher and higher in circles, until they reached a dirt ceiling.

Iamso predicted that Daniel's wife would be found soon. Daniel said he hoped so, and pushed against the ceiling. Dirt rained down. Rocks fell and clanged off the staircase.

Easy, said Oliver, rubbing his arm.

Daniel moved his hands until the dirt shifted to the side and a crack of light cut in. Dirt, rocks, worms, a section of rusted pipe, all loosened and fell. Daniel counted to three and pushed. The door flung open to a blinding orange sky and the smell of wet forest.

I saw myself pull myself up from the door in the grass.

Pillows Made of Leaves

There was a tipi and a campfire gone to ash. I was a skeleton with Hurricane-sad eyes. The sky coughed fog, and I ran inside the tipi to hide, but the air was so cold in there that I came back out and apologized to Iamso and Oliver.

We should sleep, said Iamso. I can't remember the last time we slept.

Do you ever think about Peter, asked Oliver. I always felt sorry for him with those teeth of his.

Iamso gathered leaves and formed pillows for us.

The breeze turned into a strong wind that shut my eyes.

I think about him, I said. And the two-second dreamer stuck in an endless series of dreams he can never tell anyone.

A tree broke in half, and we crouched, heads between our legs, terrified of the Hurricane. Iamso clutched a leaf pillow against his chest that fell apart in the wind.

No one knows what the Hurricane is or isn't.

The air went still. Iamso built larger pillows from the fallen trees. It was time to sleep for the first time in what felt like weeks, even though I knew I couldn't sleep, because there was a Hurricane out there and my wife, too.

I didn't say anything about Karen Suppleton and her love of McDonald's or the oil to come, because I didn't want to think about that, I didn't want to think about that anymore, because I was forgetting it all.

Karen

The first time I thought something was truly wrong with Daniel wasn't even the first time he mentioned the Hurricane. He'd disappear for hours, sometimes days, and he always had an excuse. It was always work-related, or his mother was back in the hospital, *so sick I should see her*, or just *I need a day to clear my head.*

No, the first time I thought something was really wrong was during a dinner out. Daniel had excused himself to the bathroom and was gone nearly twenty minutes. When he came back, I asked what took so long. He said he had bumped into a man from work, Peter, and they talked about tomorrow's shift.

"I never meet your co-workers," I said, looking around the restaurant. "Point him out to me."

"His table is near the bathrooms," said Daniel.

"Well, can I meet him?"

"If you want. But he's probably eating."

Something about the way Daniel dismissed me, or maybe his complete lack of interest, angered me. He wasn't always like that. When I first met Daniel, I was attracted to how passionate he was. And kind. On our second date, we went to the park, and a young girl was carrying a dying cat, and when Daniel asked if he could see the cat, the girl threw the animal skyward. The cat landed and sprinted away, and I watched Daniel run after it, across a street and behind a home with green shutters. Ten minutes later he reappeared holding the cat. We spent the next hour at an emergency vet center, where the cat was put to sleep. I remember Daniel not crying exactly, but very emotional, and it exposed a tender side to him that I was drawn to. That was old Daniel.

"I'd like to meet him," I said.

"Well," said Daniel, "you can't miss him. His teeth are all messed up. He's handsome, right, but the teeth are tough to look at."

"Are you going to introduce me or not?"

Daniel put his fork down with a clang and finished chewing. He took three quick sips from his water. "Like me, he probably just wants to eat his dinner."

I pushed my chair back from the table, and the quick screech—wood on wood—turned heads.

"Fine, fine," said Daniel. "Go talk to him. Go right ahead. I'm staying here, though."

Daniel said something else, like, "Don't do this, don't interrupt a guy that I just interrupted after his food was just served," but I didn't listen. I walked to the back of the restaurant where the bathrooms were, and there, at a corner table, was a man cutting up his food into miniature bites. His hair was blond and finely parted, and yes, he was very handsome.

"Hi, so sorry to interrupt," I said. "My husband, Daniel, said you work with him, and I wanted to say hello. I never get a chance to meet his co-workers."

"Daniel," the man looked up and said.

I didn't expect it, but close up his mouth was a poorly drawn opening, a cruel and comical shape that appeared to contain few teeth.

"Peter, right," I said. "It's nice to meet you."

"I have no idea what you are talking about," said the man. "I just want to eat my dinner."

When I went back to Daniel, he was looking over the check. I knew that something was wrong with Daniel, but I didn't want to bring it up then. At the time it didn't feel right. So I went along with his world.

"He's nice," I said. "He says you're easy to work with."

"I don't know why he doesn't go to a dentist," said Daniel. "I keep telling him, all of us do, that it would probably be covered."

Leaving the restaurant, we saw the man getting into his car. Daniel said, "See you tomorrow," and the man didn't wave but held up a hand. I said, "Have a nice night," and Daniel put an arm around my waist.

Peter—or the most beautiful man with the world's worst teeth, as Daniel called him—popped up all that summer in different forms. Daniel saw him at the mall as a middle-aged businessman with a cut lip and yellow teeth. He was at the ice-cream hut as a child who had recently lost a front tooth. Daniel saw Peter in the homeless, the successful, and even once in my father after he had been hit in the face with a baseball during a family picnic.

From there more co-workers and people appeared. There was a boy named Iamso, a man with tattoos, and someone who could predict dreams. Daniel's work on the pipeline suffered and became a pipeline destined not for oil but for water, for a town with dried-up wells.

For three weeks we separated. I said I needed a break and that we would get back together soon. I needed space. I filled the conversation with clichés, and Daniel said okay and helped me pack some of my things.

Then he called one morning asking for "an appointment," and I went along with it, thinking at the time that maybe it could actually help Daniel. I was afraid that saying no to him would be more damaging.

When he came to my apartment, I answered, and he said he was "here to see Karen Suppleton." Like at the restaurant, and as with everything else, I played along. I fell into my old habits of taking care of Daniel. I let Daniel arrange the furniture and spoke to him in questions and pseudo–Psych 101 advice, trying not to cry or yell. This was my problem and had been my problem all during our marriage when he was slipping away. I'd either go along with whatever he said or I'd distance myself completely. No middle ground.

"I see you had McDonald's this morning," he said. "Not very healthy."

"Do you remember your wife's name?" I asked at one point during our conversation. "You mentioned that she was the one who suggested you come here."

"Helena, I think. No, Karen," he said. "I don't know, she's been missing. It's been a very difficult time for me."

My name is Karen Suppleton. And my ex-husband, mind unraveling somewhere in a forest or a new part of town he's never been in but thinks he has, is Daniel Suppleton, mind going until there's nothing left but ideas, people, cracked images to fill the well. I'm worried for him, because he's never done this before. He's never disappeared completely and given in to his imagination. I've called the police, and we're going to find Daniel and get him help.

Daniel Meets Greta and Helena

Over the side of the bridge, Daniel looked into the ocean. He thought about the village of underwater pipes. He wondered if they had enough air, food, or if maybe they were all asleep and gone. He stretched his imagination until he saw the elephant stuck again in the open pipe, and then the vision blurred out and they were across the bridge and in another land.

Two identical-looking women greeted Daniel and Iamso. They were tall, thin, with short brown hair. They introduced themselves as Greta and Helena.

That's my wife's name, said Daniel. But you're not her.

Helena smiled and did a little bow. Oh, no, she said. I'm not your wife. We just share the same name.

We need to save the village of underwater pipes, said Daniel. We need to hurry. There can't be much air left.

Don't worry, said Greta. We have multiple plans.

Greta and Helena lived in a small town with about a dozen other women. The group had tea at a teahouse called Scarlet's. To Daniel it looked eerily familiar. They sat at a corner table, and when Daniel turned around to hang his coat, he saw the ⌐⊐ symbol once again. The waitress, one who looked very similar to the one at the teahouse before, came over and took their order.

Iamso and Oliver told Greta and Helena about the town, the pipeline, the Hurricane, and the village living inside the underwater pipes.

We'll save them, said Greta.

We met a group of women, said Daniel, called the deserts.

I was part of the group, said Oliver. But only as a way to escape the village of underwater pipes. I bet everyone in there is wondering where we are. They should have made their own boat. I think they're scared of drowning. Few know how to swim.

We met a group of children the deserts called the Hurricane, said Daniel. It's all very strange and distracting, and we're running out of time.

Don't forget the underground staircase and town, said Iamso.

As he wrote in his book, Greta and Helena looked at Iamso with open snarls.

We followed the Hurricane, said Daniel, down a beautiful staircase and into a village where the deserts were killed by the Hurricane and a man named Thomas.

What are you writing, asked Helena.

Poems and letters mostly.

Oliver said, He's only a child.

How old, asked Greta.

There was silence while the tea was poured.

I'm somewhere between five and fifteen, said Iamso. No one has ever told me. I've never had a birthday.

Oliver told a story about how Iamso had come to live with him, when he was known as the man with tattoos. He said Iamso was perfect company.

I see, said Helena.

Greta nodded.

Later that morning they saw the town, which wasn't much more than the teahouse, brown shacks, and a small marketplace that sold fruits and meats.

We're hungry, said Daniel. We haven't eaten or slept.

Iamso grunted, tore out a sheet of paper from his book.

Of course, said Helena. Tonight you can stay with us, and we'll cook a big dinner. We'll stuff your stomachs full.

Greta pointed to the marketplace and said, I'm thinking chicken stew.

The rest of the day, they met villagers who wanted to help save the village of underwater pipes.

We shouldn't have come here, said Iamso. I have a strange and terrible feeling about it. I wonder if they were affected at all by the Hurricane. How far are we really from where we first lived.

Maybe we could fish it out, said a man with a black beard and a crooked nose. Just build a giant hook and hope to catch a lip of the pipe or part of the body. That doesn't sound too hard if we worked together.

It's a big village of underwater pipes, said Daniel. A hundred people could be inside it, not including the animals.

Oh, said the man with the black beard and the crooked nose. We'll think of something else. I know that Greta and Helena have several ideas. He narrowed his eyes at Iamso.

I was doing so well, said Iamso. We should leave.

These people will help us, said Daniel.

They give me dirty looks, said Iamso. They don't like me writing.

We will find Helena, said Helena. And we will save the village of underwater pipes. That's what we'll do.

Search Party Is the Worst Kind of Party

A search party of volunteers dressed in brown carrying walking sticks moves through the forest looking for Daniel. There are dogs, and there is Karen Suppleton, Daniel's ex-wife, all looking for him and calling out his name.

He's out here somewhere, playing make-believe.

Inside Every Woman's Dress Pocket Is a Hammer

At night, around the cluttered tipi out here in the woods, in the cluttered home of Greta and Helena furnished with redwood furniture and carved statues of winged creatures, I talk about Peter and the two-second dreamer.

I talk about the love I have for my wife.

I talk about my love for pipes.

Then you really need to see this, says Helena.

We don't show this to just anyone, Greta says. Think of yourself as special.

They pull hammers from their dress pockets.

Above the fireplace they smash open the wall to reveal a knitting of pipes that stretch through the chimney and into the sky, where dry clouds wait for water.

I touch the pipes. Warm streams move inside.

I ask if another wall could be broken open to show my wife. Helena and Greta shake their heads no and apologize. If only, they say.

It's okay, I say. We'll find her sooner or later, and we'll rescue the village of underwater pipes for good.

After Iamso fell asleep—a moment earlier he talked about wanting to live as the two-second dreamer—Helena and Greta came into the room and carefully closed the door behind them. I stayed in bed, pretending I was asleep, opening my eyes when I thought it was safe and I wouldn't be caught.

Outside, the screams from another Hurricane being born. The Hurricane cried, pounded its tiny fists on the ocean, and stained the sky black with its breath.

Inside, Iamso slept curled on a small bed, his back pressed against the wall, his arms clutching a blanket.

Crawling on all fours, Helena and Greta groped at the floor with their hands.

Keep looking.

I am looking. I didn't say I would stop looking.

There is at least one. Most likely two or three.

In the corner, three books tied together with twine.

Got 'em, said Greta.

Helena and Greta left the bedroom, careful again with the door that squeaked.

I slipped from my bed and silently followed them back into the living room.

Near the fireplace Helena and Greta untied the books and flipped through their pages.

I thought, My tipi is a paper house filled with many homes.

Into the fire went the books.

I crept back upstairs and into the bathroom. I ran a bath for myself. Anytime I got nervous, Helena—or was it

Karen—told me to take a bath. The flames from the fire-place heated the pipes above with hot water that rushed into the tub.

Karen

I'm going to find him.

That's what I write on my left hand in black ink as the first drops of rain come down. Voices from the search party behind me. A dog runs past and chases a squirrel up a tree. In the distance a wave of leaves moves behind swaying trees, and I remember the night Daniel shook in bed. Leaves moved outside the window then, and they're moving now.

"Shut the window," he said.

"Hold me," he said.

"Stop the wind," he said.

There were many nights like that, until I couldn't take it anymore.

"When will I die?" he asked.

I'm going to find Daniel.

Save the Village of Underwater Pipes

The morning, the kitchen.

Helena and Greta serve Daniel a cup of black coffee.

Helena cooks bacon while Greta cleans dishes. Shortly

after Daniel takes his first sip of coffee, Iamso stands in the doorway.

Coffee, Iamso, asks Helena.

Iamso looks like a ghost, his skin pale and the color flushed from his eyes. Daniel thinks, Maybe he spent the night outside with the Hurricane, twisted up inside its arms and fighting. But his face lacks cuts.

Sit down, says Daniel. We're saving the village of underwater pipes today.

Iamso doesn't move. He looks at Daniel, opens his mouth a little, then closes it. Then he turns and walks away.

Daniel follows him into the bedroom. He sits at the edge of the bed. Daniel shakes him, but his eyes are empty. Daniels asks if he can write him a poem to show how he feels, and Iamso falls into the bed, turns away, and pulls the blanket up to his chin.

Back in the kitchen, Daniel eats breakfast. He asks Helena and Greta if they know what's wrong with Iamso. They say they don't. Helena hands Daniel a paper that says on the outside, IDEA ONE ON HOW TO RESCUE THE VILLAGE OF UNDERWATER PIPES AND FIND YOUR WIFE.

Daniel unfolds the paper and reads. Okay, he says. I'll try anything.

Iamso didn't come with us. He stayed in bed, his body and face pressed against the wall.

Oliver was with us. He said he couldn't sleep the night before, that the walls of his room were too hot.

We made a fire last night, said Helena. Sorry about that.

Do you know what a Hurricane is, asked Oliver.

Of course, said Helena, and from a dress pocket she handed him a paper.

SOME DEFINITIONS OF WHAT A HURRICANE MIGHT BE

1. Monster with sharp teeth
2. Angry children
3. A dozen layers of wind stuck together
4. Black magic
5. Godlike spirit
6. Curse
7. The horizon moving to the other side
8. Everyone's vision of death combined
9. Optical-illusion hologram
10. Mountain growing from the ocean floor to the sun

That list could be summed up in one word, said Greta. Fear.

We walked out of the town and into a field lined with rows of canoes. Next to each canoe stood a woman in a brown dress. Everyone said, Hello, nice to see you again, to Helena and Greta.

I envisioned the Hurricane shoving my wife into the waist of the ocean, her head held under, hands slapping the water into white blobs against a dark sky as fish chewed her ankles.

Feels like it could snow soon, said Oliver. Hasn't in a long time, but the air is cool enough.

The Hurricane loves snow, said one of the women standing next to a canoe. She introduced herself as Stella, showed us a tattoo on her wrist that said *HURRICANE ♥ SNOW*. Oliver showed her his tattoo, proud to do so, finally smiling, and the two talked about what they thought the Hurricane was and where it hid.

Okay, said Helena. This is very exciting, the first idea. She jumped up and down. And it's a simple one. The inside of each canoe is filled with pipes.

I peeked into one and saw an entire floor of pipes and a wooden paddle. In the middle of the canoe was a small seat above the pipes.

Once out in the water, continued Helena, we will all connect our pipes until forming one incredibly long pipe, and we'll stab the water until someone hits the village.

That's it, said Oliver. How will we know if we're hitting the village of underwater pipes and not something else.

Because, said Greta. All of us here are lovers of pipes and know what pipes hitting pipes feels like. It's very simple.

The canoe women nodded.

I thought, There will be a dull thud, followed by a gathering of bubbles on the surface that reads, YES, IT IS US YOU JUST HIT.

I thought, I want to spin the Hurricane by its legs and throw it into a mob of frozen trees.

We walked to the beach. Everyone dragged a pipe-weighted canoe by a rope. Oliver talked to Stella, brushing up against her, their trailing canoes bumping into each other. Helena and Greta said if this didn't work, they had more ideas. No one talked about Iamso. Some-one asked how many people lived in the village of under-water pipes.

A whole town, a forest, a hundred people or more, I said over my shoulder. An ape with a piece of coral stuck in his shoulder. And bears and deer and children who play in a stream together. Before we left, they learned how to take small breaths so they wouldn't suck up all the air.

No one said a word more until the water reached our feet and we slid our canoes into the ocean.

I wonder where Helena is, said Helena.

Once out into the body of the ocean, all of us scat-tered across a big patch of sea, we assembled our pipes into longer pipes. I clicked six or seven sections together and placed them into the water, where I attached the rest.

One woman placed her pipe into the water, and it slipped from her hands. She yelped, looked for the gone-away pipe, and sat back in her canoe, arms folded across her chest. Then, from a hip pocket, she pulled out a cookie and took a bite.

That's cookie pocket, Greta shouted at me from her canoe. You can learn about it later.

The woman finished her cookie, then pulled out an-other, and then another. With a full mouth, she studied the sky, crumbs pouring down, her canoe sailing the small hills of oncoming waves.

Another woman plunged her pipe too deep into the ocean, lost her balance, the canoe wobbled, and she fell in. It was Stella. Oliver dove from his canoe and swam in her direction. When he reached the spot where she had disappeared, he dropped below the surface, as if tucking himself into a pipe.

A minute passed. I took another stab or two at the ocean. Hit nothing.

Oliver came up with Stella, who was a blue ghost gasping for air. A Hurricane-like breeze swept across her face, and she shivered. Tilting the canoe with one hand, Oliver pulled her up and in with his other hand, placed under her armpit.

The woman with the cookie pocket paddled over and gave her a cookie.

Oliver climbed into Stella's canoe and wrung the ends of her hair dry.

Everyone else went back to poking the ocean for the village of underwater pipes. We covered a good amount of ocean but touched only water and fish.

The sky sagged and looked tired. I wanted my wife safe and asleep in the folds of the sky.

All day we paddled and searched.

Everyone in our village spent weeks preparing for a storm. I couldn't remember how many years ago. We built a wall with bags of sand and told the birds to fly away. We painted our houses neon yellow to offset the cruelty of an elephant-colored Hurricane. We painted the windows white and crossed them with wooden planks. Helena and I stood in the bedroom holding each other. I told Helena I loved her. The wind turned the walls to sand. Then we were pulled out through a white window that we forgot to cross with wooden planks.

Then Helena in the water, head held under. Me trapped under a fallen lamppost and terrified because the sky had never looked like that before. The horizon had never trembled.

I watched Helena disappear.

Once the sun's head rested on the horizon, we all broke apart our pipes and paddled back to shore.

We have more ideas, said Helena, and with her paddle she accidentally splashed Greta as she tried to be the first back to the sand.

Karen

An expanding umbrella of people looking for Daniel, we move farther into the woods. I step away from the group sweeping the woods for a body. The heroes looking for a leg in the green weeds. The heroes looking for a crumpled body against a tree. It rains and gets darker by the step.

Just be okay, I think.

"Just come to me," I say.

I walk through a clearing and find a pile of ash, what appears to be either burned twigs or feathers. I find a rusty metal pipe and part of a sandwich filled with yellow maggots.

I walk deeper into the woods, the shouts of *Daniel* bouncing from tree to tree. My feet are wet. I feel blisters forming on the soft pink skin of my feet.

I think, *I tried against something I could never change.* We had long nights, nights that began at four o'clock, where I looked into Daniel's eyes and asked him to tell me what he was feeling. He said I wouldn't understand. Later in the night, deep into the night, I'd find him sitting at our bedroom window, slumped over and sobbing. I'd watch him. He'd compose himself, open the window an inch, and stick his fingers out until it became too much, his body shaking, his hand recoiling as if electrocuted by the wind, the window slamming shut, his back curved and shoulders folding into his chest.

"Tell me," I'd say. "What's so wrong?"

"Everything and nothing," he'd say.

"It's not real," I'd say.

"Sometimes," he'd say, "the scariest part is when I can't tell what's real and what's imagination and—"

"*That* I understand. It's going to be okay."

"And the imagination is haunting, but so beautiful that I want to live in that instead."

Out here we all shout Daniel. Out here I feel like the only one who says it loud enough to tear my throat apart.

Pale Skin

The women leave their canoes in the field and walk with Daniel and Oliver into town. Daniel feels a bit defeated, and by the slow movements of everyone else, heads swaying animal-tired low, he can tell that they do, too.

In town, three men paint a house neon yellow. Others paint the windows white and cross them with boards.

Expecting another Hurricane, asks Oliver.

Anytime the wind reaches a certain height and the sky dims, we like to be careful, says Helena. The chance of the Hurricane coming back anytime soon is unlikely, but we want to be careful.

A few of the women nod. They look up at the sky and squint.

I want to see Iamso, says Daniel.

We don't need him, says Greta. He and his books were a distraction.

I like Iamso, says Oliver. I let him live with me for a while. He can tell you your feelings.

See, something like that, says Helena, is a distraction from finding the village of underwater pipes and your wife. But you can see him. No one is putting a Hurricane to your head.

Back at the house, Iamso sits crouched in the corner of the bedroom. His hair is pushed up into a frayed broom, his skin paler compared to this morning.

Iamso, says Daniel. What's going on with you.

He says, They took my books.

They say it's for the best, says Daniel.

Iamso smiles, sits back, and stretches his legs. Oliver takes a few steps toward Iamso.

Give him something to write on already, says Oliver, and from a front pant pocket he pulls out a newspaper.

Iamso's eyes light up, and Helena snatches the paper before it reaches his outstretched fingers.

No, she says. Absolutely not.

Iamso walks to the bed and buries himself under the covers, a stitched pipeline running the length of his body. Daniel and Oliver follow Helena and Greta out of the room.

Why can't he have paper, asks Oliver. Why does it even matter.

Because, says Helena. Someone who can predict someone's feelings is someone who is dangerous.

He's not a witch, shouts Oliver.

He's not a Hurricane, says a woman in a rocking chair in the corner of the room.

You want to find your wife, you want to save the village of underwater pipes, says Greta. You just want and want and want.

The woman in the rocking chair says, Don't fight. Change the subject to something nice. Tell Daniel about cookie pocket.

I'll get Stella, says Greta. It's her time of day to wear the dress.

The door opens to the sound of hammers and wind blowing leaves through the empty canals of the town.

Greta comes back into the house with Stella, who wears a brown dress. The bottom few inches are dusted with wet sand. A stitched pocket, a lighter shade of brown than the dress itself, sits awkward and visible on her right hip.

Go ahead, says Stella, try it. It's the only way to learn.

Daniel reaches in and pulls out a sugar cookie the size of his face. Oliver follows and holds up a mint chocolate chip. Both Helena and Greta pull out oatmeal raisin.

I almost drowned, Stella says. When I was underwater, I tried opening my eyes to see the village of underwater pipes, but I only saw empty ocean.

Why these cookies, asks Oliver, finishing a second.

Because that's your favorite, says Stella.

Daniel places his hand back into the cookie pocket, feels Stella's leg through the fabric, and extracts another sugar cookie. He thinks of placing the sugar cookie over his face. Sugar cookie as mask. Then he thinks of a giant glass of milk poured on his head, softening the cookie as his mouth moves.

How does it work, he asks.

There's a book, says Helena, *A Brief History of Cookie Pocket*, that explains it.

Oliver kisses Stella on the forehead, and for a moment everyone forgets about Iamso, the people without fresh air underwater, all of them getting full and drunk on cookies.

Our next idea, says Helena.

She hands Daniel another paper.

Oliver asks for milk, and he's ignored.

The paper reads, GIANT NET.

First Weather Report

```
010
TZB17 KHC 827845
WEATHER OUTLOOK
NATIONAL HURRICANE HEADQUARTERS
300 AM PDT TUE


STORM ACTIVITY . . . ASSOCIATED WITH AN AREA
OF LOW PRESSURE LOCATED SEVERAL HUNDRED MILES
SOUTHWEST OF XXX . . . REMAINS SCATTERED.
UPPER-LEVEL WINDS ARE CONDUCIVE FOR FURTHER
DEVELOPMENT OF THIS SYSTEM AS IT MOVES
WEST-NORTHWESTWARD AT ABOUT 8 MPH OVER THE
NEXT FEW DAYS. THERE IS A MEDIUM CHANCE . . .
45 PERCENT . . . OF THIS SYSTEM BECOMING A
TROPICAL STORM DURING THE NEXT 32 HOURS.
```

Giant Net

We met two identical-looking boatmen wearing suspenders on the beach. Both had black beards, black overalls, and black knitted caps. The only color they wore was their yellow boots, which rose just to their ankles.

They had created the world's largest fishing net. They explained it to me and Oliver, with Helena and Greta standing behind us listening.

On a typical day, we catch two thousand fish with this net, one of them said.

The other crossed his arms. It's such a large net we need two boats and fifteen men.

Okay, I said, let's try it.

The night before, after cookie pocket, I lay in bed. I wondered if the days would stretch out with idea after idea forever. I thought, The village of underwater pipes will never be saved. We'll die here. I thought about sneaking Iamso a book of blank paper but didn't want to jeopardize seeing my wife again.

This area of the forest, my tipi, has become a city with an ocean and people.

Two massive ships were docked side by side. The net sat on one ship in a huge pile that resembled tangled seaweed. Helena, Greta, Oliver, and I climbed aboard the ship with the net. We helped the two suspendered boatmen feed part of the net to a waiting group of suspendered boatmen on the other ship.

The net was then tied to a long wooden bar on the deck of each boat. When it was time, the ships pulled away from the dock, slowly dropping the net into the ocean. It stretched wide and low as the motors turned the water a bubbled white.

If you were standing on the shore it looked a little like this:

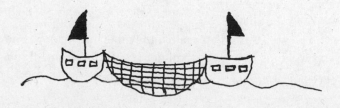

This will increase our chances, said Helena, the wind through her hair. The pipe idea was good, but it didn't cover much ocean. This net will comb more than half the ocean. Hopefully, when we get back to shore, it will contain the village of underwater pipes and your wife.

As the net dragged through the ocean, the ships slowing as they trapped sleeping schools of fish and picked crabs from the sand, Helena and Greta told us they believed in the village of underwater pipes because they lived there for a day.

We almost drowned, said Helena. Our town, like yours, flooded with ocean. If it weren't for those pipes, we'd be dead.

I remembered. On my walk through the pipes, looking for Helena, the ones playing ukulele.

I didn't ask how they left the village of underwater pipes, but they told me.

They sneaked in behind us, through the good-bye door a few seconds before the elephant was pushed out.

There was a woman there that looked like your wife, said Helena.

Where.

Exactly how you described her last night, when we ate all those cookies. My stomach still hurts. Does yours. She was in the pipe with those dangling pieces of paper shaped like creatures.

Was she alive.

She was. Curled up against the pipe, in a shadow. She was learning how to control her breathing so she didn't use up too much air.

I was there, too, in that place, I said. I must have missed her. I keep missing her.

On our way back, a boatman hollered.

The motor of the boat humming, we turned, the orange sun cutting the sails, the net below full of sea life.

The engine deepened to a growl. Boatmen on both ships waved different-colored flags to coordinate the arc of the turn, and then another long, straight line back to the dock.

All the way back, seawater sprayed my arms because I held them over the side of the boat. I looked into the splitting of the water, hoping to see a sign of life.

Caught inside the net:

1. A thousand fish
2. Crushed coral of various colors
3. Seaweed
4. Large section of pipe
5. A dead elephant

The boatmen dragged the net as far up the sand as they could. The fish took their first dying breaths of air. Helena crawled inside the section of pipe and emerged from the other side holding a dress, a lantern, and a soaked paper. Greta crouched down next to the elephant and put her ear against its mouth. She listened for a moment. Then she stood up and gave it a hard kick before noticing I was watching her. She shook her head no.

Helena held the dress. She came up to me and asked if it was my wife's. I wasn't sure. I couldn't remember.

Three boatmen turned into butchers and hacked the

elephant to chunks of meat they then wrapped in cheese-cloth they had stored on one of the boats.

I looked at the ocean and didn't see a sign of the Hurricane. The sun was a terrible orange surrounded by blackbirds. Stella joined us, and Oliver whispered in her ear. She laughed, and I couldn't understand why anyone would laugh, because everything felt so terrible.

If Iamso were here, I'd feel like this:

> *There's an image of us as husband and wife.*
> *You're gliding back away from me,*
> *hands outstretched,*
> *wearing blue overalls,*
> *your mouth an open cannon,*
> *the floor black with night and full of stars.*
> *All around us are pastel colors*
> *and trees with feathers falling,*
> *and you're gliding gliding,*
> *almost gone,*
> *your blue overalls a blue parachute,*
> *and you're floating floating,*
> *and I'm only a lover of vintage pipes*
> *and not of ladders.*

One of the boatmen ran through a water spray of flopping fish and blood. The butchers continued to work on the elephant, their cleavers raised into the sun. Another boatman ran through. They took turns trying to see who could grab the most fish on one run-through. Everyone laughed.

Well, at least it's not nothing, said Greta, now standing

next to me, watching the fish flop, the ocean ripple, the last moments of an elephant butchered. It's better than yesterday, she said.

That's true, I said. It's something.

Out and across the ocean, my eyes created an emerging mountain on the horizon. My skin sprouted dogs that ran from the beach.

That evening there was a feast of elephant meat. No one seemed to care about the elephant. Daniel thought, Iamso would care, and looked up to see him sitting vacant-eyed, ghostlike always, at the end of the table. He didn't talk. He took two bites from a carrot and relaxed into his chair. When Daniel looked away, both Helena and Greta were taking quick sips from mugs, their eyes on Daniel. He looked around the table. Oliver was touching Stella's leg beneath the table, their tattoos rubbing with each bite of dead elephant.

Old Letter from Karen

Daniel,

Last night scared me. Please don't disappear like that again. Or, if you want to leave for a while, please tell me where you are going. I at least deserve that. Did you want to talk more about what you said when you came back? What you said you saw and who you met? I believe you, you know. It's going to be okay. I could pretend to be a therapist, and maybe that would help for you to open up? Is that a stupid idea? Maybe. I just want everything to be okay, and it doesn't really feel that way. I had this horrible thought that I was going to leave you. That I couldn't take it anymore. I hope everything will be okay.

With love,

Karen

Underwater Vision System

The new morning was the same as the previous morning. A small breakfast of eggs and toast, and then Greta or Helena, whoever wasn't busy with the dishes (it was Greta today), handed me a folded paper.

It's a good one, she said. Real good.

Before opening the paper, I noticed through the single window in the kitchen, slightly above the sink, another home painted yellow. A man was crouched on the roof. He shook in a strong breeze, his knees nailed down, his arm sweeping the yellow paintbrush over the peeling shingles. Above the roof and man, a dark sky for a morning sky.

I don't know, said Helena.

Oliver came in and sat down. Don't know what, he said.

The Hurricane is threatening, Greta said. We were okay for a while there, but last night something happened. I'm sure it will be fine. The trick is not to think about it.

What does it say, asked Oliver, tapping the paper.

I opened it. It read, UNDERWATER VISION SYSTEM.

Great, I said.

Good feeling about this one, said Helena. Real good.

Do you think the people living in the pipes are still alive, asked Oliver. I mean, after all this time, all we've been through.

I don't see why not, she said. *We're* still alive.

We have to try, I said.

Karen

I've walked and shouted for Daniel for what feels like hours. I've heard thunder but haven't seen any lightning yet.

I keep thinking about the letter I put into Daniel's workbag. Not the letter, exactly, but the reason I had to write the letter.

"Daniel!" someone shouts.

I look but don't see anyone. I'm standing in a heavily wooded area of pine trees. I've walked through green swamps. As the sun sets, my arms are slick and shine with rain.

It was a night of storm, and Daniel had left the apartment, which was a first since we began living together years ago, married for two. He had begun to open the windows at night, but normally he wouldn't go out if there was even a slight wind. I waited for four hours until he came home rain-soaked and covered in mud.

At first I thought it was a good, if strange, thing— Daniel getting over his fear. But then I found him crouched in the tub, which was clogged and turning into a bath of dirt and blood from Daniel's arms.

"It's just going to happen," he said. "I saw the future me, and the future me was a mindless mess. We talked about the Hurricane gaining strength. I climbed a tree and looked for the horizon. I want to stop my job at the pipeline. I'm tired of feeling like a grunt worker assembling pipes with people I have nothing in common with. That's where it will strike. And there are levees in this town that won't hold, and a flood will come. We might be able to survive in underwater pipes. I was in the woods for a while. I lived in the woods tonight, and a tiger almost spoke."

"I believe you," I said, and got into the muddy bath.

I entered the dirty water, the colony of Daniel's fears, and ran a cloth around his shoulders as I kissed the top of his head, saying, "Yes, I believe you."

Daniel Is a Blue Dot

The canoe women come to help. A man introduces himself as Harold and explains the underwater vision system. Harold says it will work. He has found three ships and a bridge at the bottom of the ocean. Harold says the lights inside the underwater vision system are so powerful they can cut and crisscross through the ocean and illuminate everything.

We follow him to a shack on the beach. Inside, large pipe-shaped objects with glass ends.

They don't weigh much, says Harold. Don't worry about that.

He unrolls a map across a wooden table.

So everyone splits up, spreading over the ocean, he says. Each blue dot is one of you, see here. Once out on the water in your canoe, near your assigned blue dot—again, see here—you jump in the water with your underwater vision system. You don't have to stay very long, maybe a minute at the most. We don't want anyone to drown. The most important thing is, everyone is underwater at the same time and they are all moving their underwater vision system, like this.

Harold is a small man. He holds the underwater vision system, which looks like a miniature lighthouse, at his stomach and twists his hips.

Everyone paying attention, he says, moving from side to side. Very easy. Just like this. Just how I'm doing it.

Got it, I say.

And that's it, he says, placing the underwater vision system back on the table where the map is. There's a button to turn it on and off on the side. And a strap, see here, to hold it against your stomach so it's secure. And yes, everyone gets goggles, too. Lucky you.

We paddle out into the ocean, this time armed with underwater vision systems instead of really long pipes.

Helena is wearing the dress she found in the pipe. It could be my wife's. Helena has cut her hair short like my wife's. She waves at me as we paddle out.

My assigned blue dot is a far corner away from everyone else. I wait for Harold to raise a white flag to say it's time.

I sit in my canoe, the ocean waves pushing me back toward the shore, forcing me to paddle back out.

This time I'm sure of it, there, on the horizon, a new mountain. Its green point enters the air that the sky owns and the Hurricane whips.

Back on the shore, a group of people in yellow shirts wave at us. They hold signs that say GOOD LUCK ON IDEA NUMBER THREE.

Harold waves the white flag. I sit on the edge of the canoe, this silly contraption held tight against my stomach, and lean back until I fall into the ocean.

Underwater, I run my hand over and around the side of the pipe shape for the switch. From the others, beams of light flash across my face, cut through the ocean.

Click.

What Harold has invented is quite good. All of us, the blue dots, bob up and down, and people come up for air now and then. Dozens of tunneled lights brighten the ocean, reveal everything but a village of underwater pipes.

The signal to stop is a beam of light from a red lens Harold will insert into his underwater vision system. He didn't indicate how long we would stay out in the water. He did say that if you spotted the village of underwater pipes, you were to hold the light there until someone else saw you doing so, and that person would do the same, and the next person would follow, and then the next, and so on, until the village of underwater pipes was an illumination for the boatmen to find.

We stay out for two hours. The lights move through the water, waking up sea life and killing coral that feed on darkness. No one finds the village of underwater pipes.

A red light moves slowly through the water, and up we go.

Trust us, Greta says as we drag our canoes and underwater vision systems up the beach.

Trust us, Helena says as we give a defeated Harold back his underwater vision systems.

Trust us, they continue saying as we walk back to town, leaving the canoes in the field.

My wife is gone, I say. We've taken too long. Everyone is probably dead.

No one knows for sure, says Helena. They could still have air.

We need Iamso, I say.

Iamso won't help anything, snaps Greta. Trust us, we have more ideas. Don't give up so easily.

Ahead, Oliver holds hands with Stella, and it hurts me. It hurts me to see people in love.

Karen

I could have done more. That's what I think, out here, with this search party looking for Daniel. Instead I gave up, left Daniel alone and uncared for, and who knows where he is? Somewhere, out here, lost and starving.

"I'm coming," I say into the dark forest. "I'm coming."

Fight

When we get back to town, all the houses are yellow. The sky is a black rock. Wind chases the memory of water through empty canals.

A group of men and women, maybe ten total, jump and shout for the mountain to save them. I look back at the horizon and see that the mountain has grown higher.

Iamso, Greta says. Where is Iamso.

Oliver and I follow Greta and Helena and a few canoe women who run toward the house.

A door slams, and someone pounds on a wall. I sprint through the living room. The woman in the rocking chair tells me to slow down. The pipes in the wall drip water into the fireplace.

Behind me Oliver trips and falls.

I turn into the bedroom, where Iamso, Greta, and Helena are on the floor. Iamso is being held down by the two of them. To his side a drawing of a mountain, a Λ symbol, and words I can't make out.

Outside, people scream. The group of jumping men and women gets larger as people unfold a paper and read.

What are you doing. Where did you get that paper, Helena and Greta say to Iamso as he squirms in their wrist holds.

Another paper on the floor reads, IDEA ON HOW TO SAVE THE VILLAGE OF UNDERWATER PIPES: PRAY FOR A NEW MOUNTAIN, GO INSIDE THE MOUNTAIN.

A mountain, yells Greta, who is about to say something else but can't find the words, her mouth open and gaping.

Oliver stumbles into the room.

Who gave you this paper, asks Helena.

Greta is inches from Iamso's face. Do you want to kill everyone and not save the village of underwater pipes. Is that what you want. What are you.

The Hurricane throws a handful of mashed-together birds past the bedroom window. There's a loud thud, a smashed window, and a growing-louder chant to be sent to the mountain.

I wonder if it's possible to live inside a mountain and feel safe from everything outside it.

He knows what he's done, says Helena.

He's only a child, I say. Let him go, please.

I gave him the paper, says Oliver from the doorway. Hell, I gave him an entire book.

Greta's fingers around Iamso's throat relax a little as she turns to Oliver.

Where's the book, says Helena, shaking Iamso. Where is it. Tell me.

Helena stands up, and Greta's fingers tighten again. She flips the bed up, and two suspendered boatmen come into the room, armed with pipes, and smash apart the furniture and break open the walls.

Show it to us, says Greta.

Oliver holds a small knife at his side.

Where, says Greta, who picks Iamso up by the shoulders and slams his head down with such force that a floorboard cracks. Blood fans out from his head. Tell me where.

Screaming, I run at Greta.

I knock Greta over.

She smells like ocean, sand, and elephant meat. I try to pin her to the floor with my knees on her biceps while she claws at my eyes.

Oliver moves toward a turned-around Helena. Stella comes into the room yelling and tells him to stop, just everyone stop. She helps Iamso to his feet, and Greta is stronger than I thought, but I almost have her under control when one of the boatmen shoves me off and into a crumbling wall.

Helena turns, sees the knife, and hits Oliver flush in the face with a pipe. A palmful of teeth empties from his mouth, and he collapses.

The room fills with more bodies, more mouths shouting. Some people stand there yelling just because other people are yelling. A whole room of yelling people and a Hurricane outside sneaking up on us.

I see the boatmen reading the paper with the idea to pray for the mountain. Their expressions are different when they look up at Greta and Helena.

Into the room more of the canoe women. They're wearing these shirts. They triple up on Greta and Helena and twist their arms behind their backs and wrestle them from the room.

The room clears, and it's me, Iamso, Oliver, and Stella.

Iamso points outside to more people wearing these shirts that Harold is passing out. Written in charcoal is NEW MOUNTAIN, and above, in thick charcoal, Λ. The shirts look like this:

The women wear them over their dresses. The men over their button-down shirts.

Can you tell me something, I ask Iamso.

Iamso looks young and old, big and small. Of course, he says.

What am I feeling.

He takes a pipe and sticks it under an exposed lip of floorboard. A foot on one end of the pipe, he steps down and peels the floorboard from the others. A book is under the floor. Iamso grabs it, then a pencil, and writes something. There's blood drying in his hair.

He shows me the book.

That's exactly how I feel, I say. Thank you.

Something crashes into the window. It's another mash-up of birds. The crowd outside is a mob. There's the canoe women, the boatmen, who are now wearing the shirts, and Harold, all fighting with Helena and Greta, dragging them out of the town and maybe through the woods and the field and to the ocean, where their dresses will be weighed down with rusty pipes and boulders. They will be told to march in, and there will be no ukulele players for them. They had their three chances to find the village of underwater pipes and failed. Greta's and Helena's final thoughts will be the desire to hold their breath long enough to find the village of underwater pipes, a door opening and welcoming them in before they drown.

I walk outside with Oliver, Iamso, and Stella. We jump with the mob chanting for the mountain to save us. It's the only thing that *can* possibly save us. It's the only thing near and visible. It's something new, and it's something to believe in.

Hurricane, come and take us there.

Hurricane, come and displace us with the village of underwater pipes, my wife, a new life, on the rising green point of a mountain.

Karen

Roy Hassell-Thompson is the point person for the search party. He has experience in these matters. Before I went out, Roy asked me a series of questions, because he said it was standard protocol.

"Now, normally we discourage family and loved ones from being part of a search party," he said. "I understand that as Daniel's ex-wife you're upset and want to find him, but sometimes it's not always the best idea to have someone so emotionally invested."

"I'd think the opposite," I said. "I know him better than anyone else. What's the worst that could happen?"

Roy took a deep breath, leaned back with his hands on his chest, and came forward again. "I won't share the statistics with you, Mrs. Suppleton, but a case like Daniel's, someone like Daniel, missing for ninety days . . . Do I need to continue?"

"I'm going," I said.

"Do you understand what I'm saying? That when we're out there, the possibility of finding Daniel? If we find him, that he may not be alive?"

"I need to go," I said. "I understand what you're saying."

From where Daniel's car was found on the side of the road, Roy had us fan out into a five-mile radius.

All I want is to see a tent in the distance.

I hear people shout Daniel's name, and one person shouts "Danielle" by accident.

I feel like I've walked ten miles.

The wind is a giant mouth opening and expanding, and Roy blows a whistle.

Daniel Wanting to Be Safe

Iamso spent the rest of the day writing. He wore one of the shirts that said NEW MOUNTAIN with Λ above it.

Even though it was free, Iamso said he bought it with a sandwich.

It didn't feel right, he said, just taking something like that.

The town was split in half. One half scared of the Hurricane and the other half chanting for the mountain. One half jumped and formed a point above their heads with their arms and hands. The other half rocked in a fetal position and mumbled that the Hurricane would flood their stomachs. Then they changed viewpoints. One half pulled their skin to the sides of their faces with their hands and shook their heads no no no. The other half jumped with arm-and-hand-formed points over their heads, chanting for the mountain to save them.

Someone in the distance screamed my name. It was Oliver, and I asked him what he wanted.

What, he said.

You yelled my name, I said.

From behind him I continued to hear my name. I saw a group of mountain lovers jumping and told them to please stop saying my name.

A breeze carried a pyramid made of rocks into the sky and placed the pyramid on a cloud.

What town am I in. Why do I keep hearing my name. I noticed how skinny I was. My ribs showed, and my stomach was a hollowed-out bowl. I scratched my face and felt gnarled hair. Iamso told me it would be okay.

The bright yellow of the homes dimmed with the layering of clouds.

(((Daniel)))

(((Daniel)))

(((Daniel)))
(((Daniel)))
Please stop. I'm safe here.

Second Weather Report

AT 100 PM PDT . . . 400 MML . . . THE CENTER OF
HURRICANE DANIEL WAS LOCATED NEAR LATITUDE
XXX . . . LONGITUDE XXX. DANIEL IS MOVING WEST-
NORTHWEST AT 6 MPH . . . THIS GENERAL MOTION IS
EXPECTED TO CONTINUE THROUGHOUT THE DAY. A TURN
TOWARD THE WEST AND WEST-SOUTHWEST IS FORECAST
TOMORROW ALONG WITH AN INCREASE IN SPEED.

| *147*

MAXIMUM SUSTAINED WINDS HAVE INCREASED TO NEAR
114 MPH . . . WITH OCCASIONAL HIGHER GUSTS.
DANIEL IS A CATEGORY THREE HURRICANE WITH
POTENTIAL TO REACH CATEGORY FIVE.

Daniel Readies for the Hurricane as the Search Party Gets Close

It's raining. Here it comes, the Hurricane.

Everyone is back from forcing Helena and Greta into the sea.

Harold tells me he never wanted to create the under-water vision system, because he thought it would ruin the ocean with light.

((((((Daniel))))))

((((((((Daniel))))))))

((((((((((Daniel))))))))))

((((((((((((Daniel))))))))))))

That's too bad, I say to Harold.

For a moment I can see through Harold.

I'm losing my mind, I say. I'm hearing voices.

My underwater vision system destroyed the ocean like the Hurricane destroys sky, says Harold.

We need a new sky like we need a new mountain, someone says.

A new definition of fear, another says.

Yeah.

Yeah.

The wind grows with the mountain.

Soon the ocean will empty itself into this town. Giant waves will crash through the forest, trees will become floating logs with the canoe women holding on and madly trying to carve out places to sit with sharp pipes. The waves will blast off rocks and erupt into clouds. Winds will be strong enough to carry the water to a horizon so far away that it will create snow.

A second Hurricane. A second chance to save the village of underwater pipes. Who knows where it will be tossed, thrown, people as corpses or people napping. I want so many people to be alive it burns my chest. I want a chance to find my wife again. I want you to stop calling out my name.

Someone wearing one of the New Mountain shirts breaks away from the group and says, The future belongs to children, then goes back to the group. They form a long line, all of them with arms and hands formed as points raised above their heads. They snake their way through the town and sing a song for the mountain.

> *Hey, you mountain!*
> *We be comin' by a Hurricane fountain!*
> *Ha-Ha Ho-Ha, mountain!*
> *We gonna be sumptin'*
> *We gonna love you, big mountain!*

Voices, from the woods, keep coming.

I'm breaking apart from loneliness, and the Hurricane isn't even here yet.

Karen's Desperate Screams for Daniel

I decide to ignore Roy's whistle, because I know what it means. He went over it during the talk he gave us before heading out.

"And lastly," he said, "if you hear a loud whistle, it means to find me."

"Find you for what?"

"Anything," he said. "Usually it means we need to turn back."

I see dozens of volunteers move toward the sound.

Thunder and lightning cover the sky, and the rain is heavy. I yell for Daniel. When I turn around, through the nakedness of the bottom pines I see the search party putting on rain ponchos and turning on flashlights.

It's only a thought I have, bracing myself against a tree because the wind is that strong, but the thought is, *Maybe Daniel was right.*

I move deeper into the woods, shouting, not wanting to give up because of the weather.

Dannnnnnieeeellllll

DAAANIEL

DANNNNIEEELLLLL

DANIIIELLL please

Daaaaniel

Daniel

Daniel

I Am Right Here

My name is Daniel. My wife is missing. There's a chance she's in the village of underwater pipes.

A new Hurricane is coming. We're waiting for it, staring at the swirling black sky.

Then I hear it again, my name.

Daaaaannniiiellllll.

Iamso, I say. Do you hear someone.

No, says Iamso, I'm sorry, but I don't.

Who is that, I say, pointing to a woman walking from the thick of the woods into town. She's not wearing a shirt. Someone should get her a shirt.

I've never seen her before, says Iamso. She must be new.

The rain is so heavy it hurts.

Daniel, the woman screams. Daniel.

That's me, I say. I'm right here. Here I am. You can stop saying my name now.

Be careful, I think. A Hurricane is coming.

Karen

Through a curtain of black rain, I see someone. I run a short distance, leaping over a pile of brush I nearly trip on. When I'm close enough, I stop and hide behind a tree.

Standing in a small clearing, I see a tent, dozens of

sticks stabbed into the dirt, and Daniel. He's naked and covered in mud, his body a skeleton clinging to skin and a heavy beard.

"That's me," he says. "I'm right here. Here I am. You can stop saying my name now."

Daniel.

I walk up to Daniel and ask if he knows who I am.

"I don't," he says. "But you look a lot like someone I knew before. You probably lived at the bottom of the staircase."

"The staircase?"

"Maybe you didn't," he says.

"What staircase?"

Daniel walks around the sticks, says hello to one of them, and then kneels on the ground. The sky is a well of water about to empty. Daniel thrusts his fists into the dirt and then acts like he's pulling something up and open.

"There," he says, his hands holding dirt. "That's the staircase that leads to another town. You wouldn't believe it, but a group of deserts was killed by a bunch of children down there. And you should see the water system they have. It's amazing."

"Daniel," I say. "Why are you out here?"

"Who are you again? Why are you asking me these questions? Does it matter how I got here? I was in charge of building a pipeline to the ocean for drinking water, but then a Hurricane came. I lived underwater inside a village of underwater pipes for a while before escaping with a group of women called the deserts. I just told you about them, didn't I? Then I came here, where Greta and Helena had ideas on how to save the village of underwater pipes, but none of them worked, and they were very cruel to Iamso." He pointed to a stick. "And now, as you can clearly see, another Hurricane is coming. I'm not scared anymore. I'm happy it's coming, because I believe we'll end up on that mountain over there, possibly with the village of underwater pipes all washed up. That's what I want to happen, so it most likely will happen."

"Daniel," I say, because it's the only thing I can say.

I look at the sticks and notice there are names written on them: Iamso, Oliver, Stella, Canoe Woman (this one written many times), Harold. There's also a pile of sticks laid on the dirt with names: Greta, Helena, Isabella, Kimberly, Peter, Two-Second Dreamer, Thomas, are some that I read.

When Daniel turns to take one of the sticks out of the dirt and move it a few feet, I notice a massive bruise and inside the bruise a round of rotting flesh.

"Daniel," I say. "Your arm."

"I know, I know," he says. "I got hit with a pipe. It's nothing too bad."

The wound is red and wet and dotted with yellow pus.

"I thought I was losing my mind," he says. "I kept hearing people shout my name but couldn't see anyone. But it was just you."

For a moment we stand looking at each other, and I don't recognize my ex-husband.

"You need a proper shirt," he says, and runs into the tent.

When Daniel comes back out, he's holding a rag, and written on it with black pen is NEW MOUNTAIN and a triangle.

"Here, you should put this on if you want to be with the others," he says.

Daniel Sees Karen but Doesn't Recognize Her

I thought the woman from the woods was from the bottom of the staircase, but she said she wasn't. We stood in the rain, and I told her everything that happened to me. She smelled familiar.

I just want to be okay, and I know I'm not.

The woman asked about my arm, and I told her I got hit with a pipe.

I gave her a shirt to wear.

From behind her I can see more people coming from the woods. They wear plastic sheets and hold miniature underwater vision systems. They know that the Hurricane is coming, like I do.

Karen

I want to tell Daniel who I am, but I'm too scared. I'm trying to get the courage to tell him. The wind is so strong it nearly knocks me over. The rest of the search party comes up behind me with flashlights, and three or four of them grab Daniel by the arms. One of them tends to Daniel's gash with gauze. Roy is shielding his face from the wind and rain and says we need to head back and get Daniel to a hospital.

"But a Hurricane is clearly coming," I say.

"What? What did you just say? We need to get Daniel back," says Roy. He's yelling into a cell phone that they have found Daniel. People hug, and two men high-five each other. A young boy with blond hair and perfect teeth pumps his fist into the air while screaming, "Yes! Yes! We did it!"

Daniel looks worried, and when he sees me again, I want to believe he sees someone he loves.

A young girl who is going through his tent comes out with a book titled *Iamso*. She laughs and says that we won't believe the stuff he has written.

Oh, Daniel.

Daniel tells me to look for the mountain, and in the distance I can see it, I'm sure of it. I tell him yes, sure, I see a mountain.

"What else?" he says.

I see past him, and it looks as if the ocean is moving toward us. It looks like a flood, a storm, a Hurricane.

Daniel Fights a Hurricane

Then the points collapsed, and everyone screamed. Some smiled at the hopeful thought they would be taken to the mountain.

The sea moved into the woods, and the water level rose up the tree trunks, turning them blue, then black. The trees collapsed, a big wooden wall, trees hoping they would at least land on the dirt floor they had looked at for a hundred years. Then trees drowning in the rushing water that came once again through a town Daniel wanted to call home.

Look for the village of underwater pipes, Iamso said, waiting for water to hit.

People chanted to be carried to the mountain. Some sat in canoes. Oliver and Stella held each other on a raft that waited for water. Others climbed atop their yellow homes with the rats and waited on the roofs.

Daniel saw the mountain as full grown, as a green and rocky mass of land that had never been touched.

He thought, This woman here looks a lot like my wife did.

The trees passed around them. One smashed into a home. A few people shrugged, and a man with a whistle used his whistle.

It was the next wave that lifted the homes from the soil, pushed everyone into an endless somersault, water swallowing all, Daniel trying to keep his eyes open to spot the village of underwater pipes.

At one point Daniel broke the surface and saw people in canoes paddling toward the mountain. Others floated on the roofs of homes. Drowned and bloated bodies served as flotation devices. There was a helicopter, and inside the helicopter a man with a video camera.

Weather Report Is Right—Hurricane Hits

A rush of water came through the forest. Before going under, Karen saw a helicopter pass overhead. Inside the helicopter a cameraman named Shawn Stavisky captured the ocean seeping through the city and destroying the pipeline filled with oil. The shortest homes drowned. People fought against the current and struggled to reach the rooftops of tall buildings. A million spirals of oil entered the ocean.

Daniel Imagines Himself to the Mountain, a Rooftop of Safety

The Hurricane pushed me through an endless ocean. | *159*
Everything went dark. Iamso's fingers dug into my stomach. I swallowed a fistful of salt water.

I hit my head on a rock or a piece of coral. Iamso's hands lifted from my body. He was trying to say something, or was it only bubbles being blown into my ear. I couldn't tell. It sounded like someone yelling underwater. GAAAARRRRLLLLLLLAGGGGGGGGG.

Back on the surface, I opened my eyes and saw fewer canoes, fewer roofs, more floating bodies, and fewer people holding on to them. There were puddles of shirts, a darker sky.

Another wave crashed, and I was pushed down again. The water had turned ice cold. For a moment I saw Iamso, and again I thought I saw him writing. The water became shallow. There was coral.

A final series of waves formed hills in the water that we rolled over until we were pushed up against a beach, a mountain above. We were pulled back again with the now-subsiding waves on the sand, a gentle rocking, an odd weakness now to the Hurricane, my body scraping against the sand. The ocean crawled back into the horizon, and the Hurricane slinked away. The waves became smaller and smaller until there were none. We stood at the base of a mountain and watched the clouds break.

Television Broadcast of Hurricane

Shawn Stavisky captured the movement of the Hurricane from the ocean, through the woods, and into the city. His camera showed everyone outside the Hurricane, people scrambling up onto homes and drowning.

Early in the broadcast, viewers watched the ocean move closer and closer to people standing in the woods. One of the people had been identified as Daniel Suppleton, who had been missing for quite a while. People sat in front of their television sets clutching their faces as the camera panned back and forth from the water to where the people stood. Then they disappeared, and the helicopter pulled away into the heavy winds.

Daniel

Around the base of the mountain were pieces of pipe draped with seaweed and shirts. Bodies and canoes were stuck inside the pipes. Some people wrung their clothes out, stood nude and dazed. The ape with the coral stuck in his shoulder rumble-walked around a side of the mountain and disappeared.

Oliver was here. So were Peter and the two-second dreamer. They crawled out from inside one of the pipes, and each took a deep breath. Their stomachs and chests gathered air like parachutes. They coughed, exhaled dust and black clouds.

Boy, did I miss air, said the two-second dreamer. How long was I sleeping. What did I miss.

Peter cried while laughing. His teeth looked shattered. He spit blood and wiped ocean and Hurricane from his face with his sleeve.

Where is Stella, asked Oliver. Has anyone seen Stella, he said to everyone, who responded, I don't think she made it.

He asked the canoe women, and I couldn't hear what they whispered, but one of the whispers knocked him to the ground. Iamso ran over, wrote him a poem, and the two sat together for a minute before walking back to where I, Peter, and the two-second dreamer stood.

You're alive, I said to them. You're really alive.

Of course, they said. We didn't breathe much in there, but we're alive.

You don't need much air, said the two-second dreamer.

I always thought I needed so much, just living outside, but not really.

How do we get inside it, said Iamso.

Inside what, asked Oliver, who rubbed his tattoo and looked at it closely, as if it could flake off.

If it's a new mountain, everything inside it will be new and ours, Iamso said.

I asked Peter and the two-second dreamer if many people had died. They said a few. They told me to look around. Most of the original town was here. Some had broken bones, cuts, bruises, but they were all here. Their eyes looked dark and sunken. I didn't see my wife.

Iamso was eager to find a way into the mountain. I said we could start our lives over here. Iamso agreed and said once we found a way into the mountain, it would be the perfect hiding place from any future Hurricanes.

How did you guys survive, said Oliver, sitting down on the wet sand, patting the healing wound on his face with the tips of his fingers.

Peter looked at Oliver's teeth and sighed. He picked up one of the New Mountain shirts and tied it around his mouth and face, only his eyes visible. Surviving was easy, he said.

I was in a coma, said the two-second dreamer. Basically dead.

There wasn't anything to do but sit and talk, continued Peter. We trained our stomachs to digest salt water. We ate dead animals, most of which died from a lack of fresh air and forest. People thought I was dead at one point because I was so quiet. I slept, mostly. We used less air.

Did you see my wife, I asked. She might have been sleeping near the section of pipe with the folded paper animals hung from the ceiling.

No, said Peter, I didn't.

It was a perfect place to hide from the Hurricane, said the two-second dreamer.

It was, said Peter. It was like that cave I showed you, but underwater.

We walked around the mountain. The Hurricane had swallowed everything up. I looked out at the horizon and looked for old lands, any land, the bridge, the first home where all this began, and saw only water. Iamso said this was it, the final place left to live, and we should begin building homes.

The top of the mountain coughed up a plume of smoke. Iamso wrote in his book, and it looked like this:

We made one full circle around the mountain and came to where we started—the ruins of the village of underwater pipes, our old town, fallen trees—scattered across the sand. Canoe women sat without canoes, looking at their bruised legs.

The Hurricane had left behind a summer heat.

One of the men said that if we were looking for a door

to the mountain, we had already missed it. Iamso asked what he meant. He pointed at the mountain. Right there.

On the mountain someone had painted a yellow door, the same color as the homes. At the bottom of the door, written in black charcoal: I DON'T BELIEVE IN A HURRICANE ANYMORE, the bottoms of the letters cut off by the mountain dirt.

You did it, said the man, and he pointed to Iamso. I saw you. Before anyone else woke up, you did it.

Iamso wrote something in his book and then looked up at the man.

I guess I forgot, said Iamso.

Well, does it work, asked Peter.

Another plume of smoke rose from the top of the mountain.

164 | It was silent without the Hurricane. The light splashing of waves could be heard behind our ears as we walked up to the door painted on the mountain.

I couldn't find my book, Iamso whispered in my ear. Everyone was still unconscious from the Hurricane, and I couldn't find my book, so there were these buckets of paint, and I figured I would just use that.

Oliver separated us by pushing and walking between our shoulders. At first he tried to pull the door open by digging his fingers inside the edge. When that didn't work, he pushed the door with one hand, and it swung open.

It works, someone said behind me.

Inside the mountain was a long, hot tunnel. I imagined a sun inside the mountain. I, Iamso, Peter, the two-second dreamer, and a few others—canoe women,

men from the town—all walked together and into the mountain.

The walls were lit by white light. The heat placed beads of sweat on our skin and dried our clothes with each step as we moved through the mountain.

Have you given up on your dream of finding Helena, asked Iamso.

Maybe, I said. I don't know what to believe anymore. I was once a plumber. I'm not even sure Helena is her real name.

I'll write more poems about you, said Iamso. That will help.

Oliver asked if anyone thought we could live here. There were no animals or plants. It was too hot, someone said. It was safe, but we couldn't survive without food and water for very long. Iamso said we could build a pipeline again, filter the water, and use the mountain for a hiding place if the Hurricane came back.

But there's no food, said the two-second dreamer.

Fish, I said. We can eat fish. We still have canoes. And if we're lucky, we can walk back around the mountain and check for plants. We can grow things. We can try. This is a beginning.

At the end of the tunnel, we came to a wall. There was no yellow door painted to get out. We turned around and walked back outside. Peter gently closed the door and said it reminded him of the cave.

Everyone agreed the Hurricane would come back again. But we now had the mountain on our side.

Oliver made fishing poles and taught the canoe

women how to catch fish, which they already knew how to do.

They paddled out into the evening sea and came back minutes later with a hundred fish that Peter cooked on the fire that Oliver had made from branches.

At night we decided to sleep in the mountain. We felt safer. Before falling asleep I imagined creating a new yellow life here. We'd plant trees and cut the trees down for homes. And then we'd plant more trees for more homes after the canoe women gave birth to screaming babies.

I saw myself circling the mountain until a field of horses, cows, chickens, and pigs appeared. I wore a shirt that said WE CAN LIVE HERE NOW, and Helena was here even though it wasn't really her but a new Helena. We can live here now, I mumbled in my sleep.

In the morning three of the first pipes, the very largest pipes, had washed up on the mountain shore. Inside were more parts of our original town. There were ladders, pipes, half a house, a farm of animals, trees, birds, a road of dirt, wagons, a door, magnifiers, lanterns, seeds, wagons, potatoes, a violinist, and a man who called himself a villain who laughed and immediately ran inside the mountain.

Well, he's a strange one, said Oliver.

For the next two weeks, we built our town. I spent most of my time walking around the mountain, using a ladder and a magnifier to look out into the sea. There was something terrifying and exciting about knowing that we were the only ones left. That the Hurricane had swallowed up everything else. I wondered what was under the ocean. I wondered if the Hurricane would come back and if the mountain could stand up to it.

After the town was done, I picked a new Helena, a new wife. All the canoe women stood in a line, and we held an audition.

Are you sure about this, I asked Oliver and Iamso. I'm really not sure about this.

All you ever wanted was your wife back, said Iamso. And that can't happen. But everything is starting over, and you can have a new Helena. That can happen.

Are we going to die, said Peter, looking for the Hurricane in the sky, hiding behind a cloud or the sun. When the wind came, he trembled and crouched in a position with his arms tightly wrapped around his legs.

Each of you, said Iamso to the canoe women. One by one, please come up. Give Daniel a hug, whisper one sentence of compassion in his ear, and then kiss him on the cheek.

Even the air smelled new here. Heat evaporated from the mountain. New clouds squeezed from the tip of the green peak and floated into the Hurricane-washed sky.

The first woman hugged me very lightly. She whispered, You are such a nice man. She kissed me near my left eye.

The second woman was a little better. She hugged me close but whispered, I will cook and clean for you every day. Her kiss hit my nose; she apologized, then she kissed my chin.

It wasn't until the second-to-last woman that I found Helena. She hugged me close, her lips traced my earlobe, and she whispered, Everything will be okay. I will keep you safe. She kissed the corner of my mouth, and she held it there.

Iamso had them participate in a footrace, a contest to

see who could hold her breath the longest underwater, and finally a three-question test called Why Should You Be the New Helena.

That one. I pointed to Helena. That's the one.

Close your eyes, said the two-second dreamer. And count to fifty.

Spin around a few times, said Oliver.

I wonder if we will all die soon, Peter said again from his Hurricane-crouched position.

I closed my eyes, and someone—I think it was Iamso—twisted my shoulders, and I spun once, then twice. I counted aloud to fifty. Other people counted with me, and it became a little song.

When I opened my eyes, Helena was gone.

Go and find her, said Iamso. She's somewhere around the mountain. Or maybe inside the mountain. When you find her, it will feel more real. It will feel like you've found your wife.

I walked through the town. Workers built homes. Iamso had written his name near the door to each and drawn a stick figure of himself.

Before leaving, everyone waved good-bye. Iamso wrote me a poem about finally finding my wife and feeling happy and loved and unafraid.

Karen

When the water came, I tried to grab onto Daniel, but I went under with the rest of the search party. I was dragged across the woods until we were back in town. The height of the water was at the throats of our homes, and people were all on their roofs screaming for help, some holding signs. I shouted for Daniel as I swam against the rushing water. A body floated past me and pushed up against the side of a home with another.

I saw two helicopters in the sky with searchlights leave everyone. The wind tilting the helicopters from side to side was maybe too much.

I swallowed salt water, spirals of oil, and tried to keep my head above the water.

I thought, *In some strange way, Daniel was right.*

I had never seen the sky so dark.

I swam toward an empty roof.

Daniel Finds His Wife

Around the mountain was mostly dirt and rock. Some trees had begun to grow from the soil we found in an old pipe. Deer ate berries from a shrub. Everything was bright and clean, and I was about to find my wife.

Helena. Helena. Helena, come out wherever you are.

I searched half a side of mountain before taking a break. I looked out into the ocean and noticed the horizon sitting low. The sun was gigantic. I stretched my legs, wrote my name with my finger in the sand, and then continued walking around the mountain yelling for my wife to appear.

I looked under rocks.

I climbed the mountain and inspected ledges.

I lifted blankets of dirt and hoped to find a sleeping Helena.

I checked the sky for the Hurricane holding Helena hostage.

I screamed for Helena to come out come out wherever you've been for the past weeks, months, years.

I came to a patch of land where there were more broken pipes scattered in a warm dirt field.

I looked inside each pipe.

Daniel, said a voice. Daniel, is that you.

It was Helena, crawling from the end of a pipe, dusting the ocean off her dress, the one I remembered her sewing under an evening sun that didn't know the various definitions of a Hurricane.

I stood up, and Helena crawled out from the pipe. She threw her arms around me and whispered in my ear, Everything will be okay. I will keep you safe, and kissed me on the corner of my lips. I tucked a strand of dirty hair behind her ear. I kissed her on the lips. I held the back of her head in my hands, and she did the same, and our foreheads rubbed against each other as the sun circled the mountain.

I'm so happy you're back, I said.

I missed so much of our life, Helena said. I'm sorry.

Everything is starting again, I said.

Did you find out what a Hurricane is.

Not really. But there is a boy named Iamso.

Maybe he could be a son. Maybe we'll have a family now.

I missed you.

I missed you.

Karen

The wind let up, but the rain was still heavy. It took all my strength to swim to a roof empty of people. I dug my fingernails into the grit of the shingles as water blasted around me. I heard a baby scream. I didn't see anyone else from the search party. I pulled myself up a little and kicked my right leg up, my foot on the edge of the roof giving me the final leverage to climb out of the ocean.

I sat on the roof, and when the wind blew, I felt a stinging pain in my neck. I touched the left side, near my shoulder, and felt my fingers sink. When I looked, my hand was covered in blood.

I took my shirt off and pressed it into the wound.

I saw nothing but drowning homes and water littered with bodies, animals, garbage, seaweed, parts of broken homes floating away from me.

I sat shivering on the roof, looking at the other roofs for Daniel. In the distance, where the water seemed shallow, a group of men were throwing television sets. Some others in a boat paddled from home to home spray-painting gang signs in neon colors.

Daniel

When we came back to the town, Iamso had written his name on more homes. A pipeline stretched into the sea. On each section of pipe, Iamso had scribbled his name. There was a water-filter machine with Iamso written on it. Scraps of paper from Iamso's notebook, the word Iamso written on them, had been nailed to trees.

I gripped Helena's hand. She kissed me quickly on the neck. Peter, Oliver, and the two-second dreamer introduced themselves.

May I, said the two-second dreamer.

Yes, I said.

The two-second dreamer lay on the ground and brought his knees to his stomach. He placed his hands under his head and was soon asleep.

There were green stars in the sky.

Oh, this is something else, said Helena.

I swung her hand a little, creating a breeze that made Peter shiver and cry.

A moment later and the two-second dreamer jumped to his feet. It's a good one, he said, and whispered the dream into Helena's ear.

How wonderful, she said.

What did he say, I asked as we followed everyone inside a house Iamso said could be ours.

I saw a field of horses, she said. It was beautiful.

We walked into the home, into a room still being built. The room was filled with beds. Four men in overalls were building a second layer to the room, which was only about twelve feet high, and they were installing more beds. There will be a ladder, one of them said. For you to climb up.

I thought you meant this would be a home for only me and Helena, I said.

No, said Iamso. For all of us. We're a family again.

Iamso had written more on the walls. Stories, poems,

letters were on everything. His hands were covered in ink.

It's all new, he said.

And your books.

I've done away with them. I'm using the town, everything now. It's called graffiti.

Helena and I sat down on a bed, following Oliver and Peter, who did the same. The two-second dreamer lay down on a bed and went to sleep.

Pretty good room, isn't it, said Iamso. The second floor will be for you and your wife.

What's graffiti, asked Helena, squeezing my hand.

Before Iamso could answer, Helena whispered in my ear and asked how old Iamso was. I said I didn't know. No one could tell.

Iamso leaned against a wall. His body shrank in the odd angles of dark light. Oliver and Peter sat close, whispering about Hurricanes.

It's a type of writing I invented, Iamso said. All this time I wrote in books. But books can be destroyed, lost, drowned, inked letters erased by salt water.

Oh, said Helena.

Iamso walked over and sat on the bed next to us, next to Helena.

I would have been forgotten, Iamso said, if it were up to Greta and Helena. When we came here, and the pipes and pieces from our old town washed up, I realized those things were forever. And I could write on things that were forever. Does this make sense. Maybe I'm not making any sense and I should let the mountain speak for me.

No, you're making sense, said Helena, who patted his head.

What about the mountain, I asked.

I wrote my feelings on the west side of the mountain, said Iamso. It's covered in paint. It's forever.

As Helena rubbed his arm, whispering and mumbling to him that everything would be okay, Iamso cried. He talked about Greta and Helena taking his books away and how empty he felt. He talked about the strength of a Hurricane and how it could swallow books whole. But not a mountain, he said. Not pipes and homes and roads and trees, he said, sitting up straight and wiping his nose with a bare forearm checkered in paint and charcoal.

Finished, said the workers above our heads. They slipped a ladder down, made of pipes, each tiny section a scribbled pattern that said IAMSO. They descended the four short rungs to where we sat.

I'll be right back, I said.

I nodded and smiled at Oliver and Peter and even to the two-second dreamer, who was asleep.

Outside, two women washed Iamso's name from a mailbox. When they saw me, they stopped, placed their cloths inside the box, and smiled, looking up at the sky. Others did the same, trying to clean massive amounts of writing that Iamso had splattered over the town.

I ran to the west side of the mountain, through a field of sun, noticed a pig with IAMSO written on his side, and headed into a block of shade on the west side of the mountain.

There, stretching from the bottom of the mountain to the peak where smoke curled out, was the writing of

Iamso. At the bottom the words I AM NOT AFRAID OF A HURRI-
CANE written multiple times. There were a few poems, a
letter to the Hurricane, and, higher above, words I
couldn't make out. It was as if Iamso had taken his books
and transcribed them to the mountain.

I spit on my hand and tried erasing the line I AM SO
AFRAID OF SOMETHING IN THE SKY from the rock. Using a
stone, I tried scratching it off. Nothing. It stayed. The
shade was cool in the shadow of the warm mountain.

Back at the house, Iamso asked me if I remembered
the picture of the pipe. I said I didn't. He showed me a
picture on the wall that looked like this:

I remember, I said. At the teahouse it was carved into
a wall. And we received a message through the pipeline
one day with it, too.

It was me, said Iamso.

But how did you put it through the pipeline, I asked.

I ran down a dozen sections of pipe and separated
two parts, placed it in, and poured a bucket of well
water in.

Well water.

Near a tree, said Iamso. In a bucket. It's where I

carved the first picture into a tree that Peter found. That's when I got the idea of sending a message through the pipeline. I didn't know what I was doing. I want to be remembered. I wish I had discovered graffiti earlier.

Oliver and Peter still sat on the one bed. They took turns predicting when the next Hurricane would hit.

It doesn't matter, said Iamso. Because if it does, we'll go ahead and move everything inside the mountain where it's safe.

I don't think it will come back, said the two-second dreamer. Remember when we lived in pipes and those women thought the Hurricane was a group of children.

I bet they drowned, said Peter.

Helena and I climbed up to our bed, above the other beds, against a wall covered in Iamso's writing.

We lay in bed and held each other. Peter guessed his death, and Oliver said something about his tattoo. Iamso talked about living forever. He said a mountain probably lived to be ten thousand years old. The two-second dreamer said he was going out for tea and asked if anyone wanted some.

I held Helena until she fell asleep. I whispered the poem to her that was painted on the wall.

Karen

Something about Daniel: For the first three months of our marriage he picked up my pajamas that I threw wadded into a ball on the floor each morning, and he untangled them, and he folded them into a neat little square, and he placed them on my pillow for that evening.

Old Note Written by Daniel but Never Given to Karen

I got your note today in my workbag and read it on my lunch break. I'm not sure what happened last night, but I wanted to say I'm sorry. I'll get help. I can fix this. You're right, you don't deserve any of this. Everything will be okay, and we will be safe, I promise. I love you a lot. It's just sometimes I can't control things. Who can? It's harder for me than other people. I'll get help. And I have you. Everything will be okay! I love you a lot.

Daniel

I woke to the sound of a crowd's roar. Helena was still asleep. I peeked out the top of the window, through the ink scratches of Iamso, and saw Iamso standing on a ladder, the town huddled around him.

Be back, I said to a sleeping Helena.

It was a hundred degrees outside, and Iamso gave a speech about destroying the Hurricane for good. Most of the men hollered and cheered. Canoe women told him to take a blanket and to be safe.

The Hurricane has retreated, said Iamso. Now is the time.

How will you do it, someone asked.

Everyone got quiet, except for a man up front who kept yelling. Iamso stared at him until he stopped.

I'll paddle out in a few hours, said Iamso, when the sun goes down. I'll go to the horizon where the Hurricane is and confront it. I'll drain the ocean if I have to. I'll write my name across the sky.

Everyone nodded. Some people shrugged and said, Not bad.

Peter stood next to me and whispered that we would all die soon.

Oliver said, We will, depending on what you think soon is.

When the sky filled with clouds, Peter clutched his mouth and crouched, his body shaking more than the new trees in the wind.

He's beautiful, said one of the canoe women, pointing at Peter.

Iamso said the Hurricane was coming again, that it somehow knew he was planning to attack it. He pulled up his shirtsleeve, his arm covered in pictures, words, cuts, bruises, and wrote his name over where his name had already been written.

We cheered and waited for the sun to touch the ocean, the shade to pull itself around the mountain like a curtain.

Helena asked what he was doing. I said I wasn't sure, but it was exciting. I told her the only thing that seemed to matter was that she was back now. She asked why the mountain kept getting warmer, and Oliver interrupted and said it was better than snow.

Peter lifted his head and was about to say something, then went back to trembling.

The sun fell fast. Helena wrapped her arms around me and whispered how much she loved me, how she was sorry she ever left in the first place, how alone she felt living in the woods where a pipeline once entered on its way to the ocean, how she thought she had seen me but didn't know for sure, how one night tigers roamed her tent.

Think of the two-second dream, I said. The field of horses.

I don't want to think of death anymore, someone shouted at Iamso.

I don't want to be scared anymore, another said.

Yeah.

Yeah.

Yeah.

That's why I'm going, Iamso said.

We stood with the mountain at our backs. Soon the sun dipped into the sea horizon, and Iamso pushed a rowboat into the water. On the sides of the rowboat, his name was written a thousand times.

We waved good-bye. Our arms were marked with graffiti Iamso. A few waved red flags. Someone whispered the hope that he would kill the Hurricane so they could live in peace. Peter, weeping with the accumulation of clouds, said that would be nice.

Iamso paddled into the sun, his body a block of shade and hope. I held Helena. She wrapped a leg around my leg and said she wouldn't leave me again.

Karen

A helicopter flies over, and I stand up and wave with one hand while keeping the other hand holding my shirt pressed against my neck, afraid to pull it away.

I look from rooftop to rooftop, because I don't want to see what's in the water that is just beginning to splash the edges of the roof.

Daniel wanted kids. I remember one night after he took a shower, he ran into the living room and said, "Let's have a baby." Just like that, out of nowhere. And I said, "We can try."

There was a point when Daniel thought he could fix himself, and there was a point when I knew it wouldn't happen. He wasn't talking much, and when he did, it was about something that didn't make sense, didn't seem real. We stopped talking about the future.

"We'll keep trying," he kept saying.

In the distance, on a rooftop, I see a man waving his arms wildly in the air, but there's no helicopter in sight. I want to believe it's Daniel.

Daniel

While we waited for Iamso to come back, the people who lived in the village of underwater pipes answered questions about how they lived. They told stories about eating animals, how the animals died after a week. Their stomachs grew accustomed to drinking salt water. They wondered how long they would live but felt oddly safe inside the pipes, inside the ocean.

The Hurricane couldn't reach us, said a man with a bushy beard and Hurricane-sad eyes. We were tossed around now and then, but it wasn't a big deal.

But you would have run out of air, said Helena, who sat between my open legs on the hot dirt.

Most likely. That's why it was lucky the Hurricane pushed us up onto this mountain.

What's on the inside of your lips, asked Helena.

The man with the bushy beard and the Hurricane-sad eyes pulled his bottom lip down and showed the name IAMSO written in black. Helena squeezed my thigh.

It got dark. Oliver lit the lanterns. Someone else made a fire, which was a bad idea because it was so hot. They put the fire out with a bucket of ocean water.

That's him, said Peter. Here he comes.

Where.

There, there, the splashing.

Over there.

Iamso.

That's not him. I don't see a thing.

I thought I saw something.

You wanted to see something.

The sky is too dark.

Someone invent a cold fire. I can't see a thing.

I think I'll write on the mountain, said the man with the bushy beard and the Hurricane-sad eyes. If Iamso can do it, I bet I can. It looks like fun.

He took a lantern, grabbed a bucket of paint, and walked over to the mountain, where he wrote, I WANT TO SEE SOMETHING, BUT THE SKY IS TOO DARK, with his fingers.

Soon the mountain would be completely covered by writing.

Maybe that's him, someone said.

Nope, that's a fish.

Anytime the water moved, someone pointed and shouted for Iamso, but it was me who saw him paddling from the horizon and through the dark waters.

I held my lantern out and walked into the water. Five people followed me, their lanterns swaying in the air. We produced a little glob of light, which Iamso entered.

His rowboat separated us and beached itself on the mountain sand. Iamso spit up a mouthful of red liquid that looked like blood. He had teeth marks on his left arm that looked like they were from human teeth. His shirt was ripped, and his hair was messed and wet.

Helena and a few others helped him from the boat, asking him if he was okay. He nodded, took a pencil from his pant pocket, and wrote something on his palm before making a fist. I'm okay, he said. The Hurricane is dead.

People looked at one another. The man yelling from before started yelling again until someone told him to just stop already.

I did it, said Iamso, struggling to hold himself up. I killed the Hurricane.

Peter pulled down the shirt he had used to cover his mouth. He smiled, and three teeth fell out. He thanked

Iamso, and soon everyone else followed. They cheered for Iamso and told him they would cover the entire mountain with his name so he would be remembered forever.

And I'd like a statue, said a weak Iamso.

Oliver said something to the two men who had built the extra floor and bed in our house, and off they went.

Helena said we could finally live in peace. That the ocean would be calm enough to make love in. We could live a long life. Someone declared tomorrow Iamso Day. A party would be held.

Karen

The helicopters are gone again, but there are more bodies in the water and more people screaming from rooftops. Below them, below me, are homes filled with ocean, closets collapsed with fish.

"Daniel!" I scream at the man in the distance on the roof. "Daniel!"

When the water gently splashes over this roof, I decide to swim to where Daniel might be. The water is barely above the front door there. It's not too far.

I tie my shirt around my neck, around the wound that stings in the salt water as I enter.

The water is calm and filled with wreckage. I swim slowly, careful not to bend my neck too far to the right.

Daniel

The statue was unveiled in the morning. Somehow it captured the odd shape and size of Iamso. Iamso himself wrote his name across the statue's face and wrote a poem down his back.

All morning, people from the town worked to write IAMSO on the mountain. They covered about half before passing out on spiky cliffs and flat ledges. When Oliver asked, What about the inside, Iamso said, Yes, write my name on the inside as well, and Oliver ran to the door painted on the mountain.

They treated Iamso like a king. They said he'd saved the village of underwater pipes and killed the Hurricane. Everyone agreed they could live in peace.

Even the two-second dreamer was under his spell, and on Iamso's command, every hour, he gave Iamso a new two-second dream. When I asked Iamso if I could do anything, he said I was good now because I had Helena and that's what mattered.

He's right, you know, said Helena, who kissed me on the neck. A party followed another party without a sign of the Hurricane, only blistering heat. The ocean was a lake, the sky an open mass of blue cradling a large sun. We swam, lay out in the sun, took turns sleeping inside the mountain.

Three days later and the mountain was completely covered with graffiti Iamso. Oliver held an audition and picked a new Stella. Peter tattooed her arm. The two men built another bedroom in the one-room house. People discussed having kids and starting families. Anytime a tree sprouted up, a rock loosened from the mountain, found pebbles littered the beach, baby hermit crabs crawled, missed corners of a bedroom were spotted, Iamso called for more graffiti Iamso and a handful of people ran with buckets of paint to write his name.

Karen

Something bites my ankle, and when I spin around, I notice a huge patch of blood on the surface of the water. There's a boat a few feet from me and bags of garbage and leaves and sections of the pipeline caked in oil, and pieces of wood and parts of homes floating.

I feel dizzy and decide to climb into the boat, which is more like a raft. I pull myself in and lie down with my head propped up against one end. Blood flows down my chest as people scream and a horn is heard in the distance. I hear a few people splashing, swimming past me. I fade out for a moment and think, *Daniel, I lost you, so please come find me.*

Daniel

A tiny factory was built, where food was produced. A baby was born to Oliver and Stella. People called themselves things like Doctor, Blacksmith, Scientist, Historian, and Cook. No one built a wall, because the threat of a Hurricane didn't exist.

Helena and I tried to have a child and failed. I told Iamso that everything wasn't perfect just because he killed the Hurricane. He agreed and said it was perfect because we don't have to live with the fear of having an unnatural death. When I asked what the Hurricane looked like—was it children, or perhaps a giant man, a monster— he said no, it was something much more terrible.

Like what, I asked.

Iamso sat with me in the house with one room. Additions had been made, so the one room was now three floors of all beds. Graffiti Iamso covered everything. People above us were sleeping.

186 |

Daniel, please come find me, Iamso said.

What.

I can't tell you what the Hurricane looked like. It's better this way, said Iamso.

And what are we supposed to do, I said. Look at everything we've been through. Things feel calm. What do we do now.

We could hold an audition for a child for you and Helena, said Iamso. A lot of people have had children lately. They probably wouldn't mind.

No, I said.

Iamso asked to see my fingers, and on each one he wrote his name in purple ink, which was a new color, invented by the man calling himself Scientist.

Everyone is happy here, said Iamso. We will all die in our sleep. There is no disease or anything to be scared of.

I asked about the mountain. The mountain had grown so warm that it was unbearable to go inside. Someone found the heat-bloated body of the person calling himself a villain.

Iamso said heat was better than cold, better than a Hurricane.

Karen

There was another occasion, early in our marriage, when we went for a walk after dinner one evening. The rain came quickly, with only the warning of several swaying trees. Daniel sat on the ground, in the road, and wouldn't move. I asked what was wrong with him and if we'd ever have a child. Cars blew their horns and swerved around us.

"You'll leave me," he said. "I can feel it."

"I'm not giving up," I said.

When the rain stopped and the sun was coming out, I said I didn't want to be with someone who acted like this. I didn't know what was so wrong with him. I said things I didn't mean. Daniel, I said things I didn't mean.

Daniel

I wondered if Iamso actually killed the Hurricane. No one knew exactly what a Hurricane was. No one had seen an actual Hurricane. Iamso killing a Hurricane didn't make sense.

I wrote on scraps of paper and, while everyone was asleep, walked through town slipping them under the doors of houses, shops, the teahouse, and the tiny factory.

What I wrote:

How do you think I killed the Hurricane. Please answer below and leave at the door to the mountain. This should not be discussed among others.

I signed it, *Iamso*.

I stayed up all night, sitting against a side of the mountain. I wondered what the sun looked like after it sank into the horizon.

Two hours later and people were dropping the scraps of paper at the door. I kept count. For a while the man who called himself Butcher didn't appear. I worried. And then he showed up with a blood-soaked paper in one hand and a small pig in the other. He left both at the door.

Iamso would be up in another hour. He slept more than anyone else. I took one last walk through the town, remembering where I'd left the papers and checking off who had come to the mountain.

I counted everyone.

I collected the papers and walked to the side of the mountain where I'd spent the night. The sun came up and cut across the water. It rose up the side of the mountain and formed a light for everyone to read the graffiti Iamso, and for me to read the scraps of paper.

Each answer was different.

What I read:

1. By talking to it and coming to a resolution—Canoe woman number five
2. By pretending it doesn't exist anymore and putting it in the past—Historian
3. With death—Multiple workers
4. You finally confronted it, nobody else would, we all hid. Now it's over with.—Oliver
5. Probably used one of my cleavers—Butcher
6. By making everything new and forgetting about the horrible past. It's all future now.—Peter
7. With a rope and the threat of draining the ocean—Tea maker
8. You didn't kill anything. You only erased the idea of the Hurricane.—Canoe woman number two

There were more. Predictions on killing methods, death threats, torture methods, and verbal-assault methods, but the last answer, by canoe woman number two, was the most interesting. I decided to wait a little, walk home, and have breakfast with Helena. We'd go for a swim to fight the heat. I'd ask Iamso if he wanted anything written anywhere today, and then I'd have tea with canoe woman number two.

Karen

A rescue boat is coming. I can hear it in the distance. It's a massive white boat with a red stripe painted on the hull. It will come through and pick up all the people from their drowning homes.

I can't move my body. I don't know how much blood I've lost.

Daniel is somewhere safe inside his imagination, and there's this small part of me that envies him. That wants to be him. There's a bigger part of me that wants to take back everything I ever said and say things when I didn't say anything and should have.

I lift my head slightly to look over the side of the raft and feel a scarf of blood pour around my neck and down my body. There are other people on rafts screaming for loved ones. One man sits on the backboard to a basketball hoop. Another lies on his side on a front door painted a neon color. The top of the water, everywhere I look, is covered with garbage. The water gets higher. I try to shout for Daniel one last time, but I can't speak.

Daniel

I approached her on the street and introduced myself as the husband of Helena.

Of course, she said. I've heard many things about you, from Helena.

I wanted to talk to you, only for a moment. Can we have tea.

Inside the teahouse I noticed that Iamso had it constructed so it looked exactly like the one in the original town. Even the server looked the same. And on the wall, where I had seen it before, the drawing of the pipeline carved into the wall.

I'll have chamomile, said canoe woman number two.

We talked briefly about the past, which she said she wasn't sure if we were allowed to do. She said how all the landmasses had drowned in the ocean from the final Hurricane, even the bridge, the clouds. She said if it weren't for this mountain, we'd be dead or living in canoes or in a village of underwater pipes where the air would eventually run out.

It's a good thing Iamso took care of the Hurricane, I said.

The server brought our pot of chamomile tea, asked if we wanted anything to eat, and went back to the bar area.

What is he anyway, she asked. A man some days and a boy the next. I don't get it.

I knew him in our original town, I said. Which looks very much like this one now, getting closer every day. Except Iamso didn't have much control then. He was only a writer of poems and letters. We went on quite an adventure.

We sipped our tea, which was served cold. It had taken some getting used to, such cold tea. It was so warm on the mountain that drinks and food were served without heat.

Canoe woman number two asked about Helena, if we planned to have kids, what the future held, if we were happy, and, finally, what I thought about graffiti Iamso.

It's strange, I said. It's everywhere. Do you ever wonder how he killed the Hurricane.

Does it matter.

I guess not.

He's made everyone calm, she said. In return we've let him write his name and words wherever he wants. It seems like a pretty good trade to me.

But you don't think he actually killed, maybe children, a man, something, a whatever-it-is.

The server came back with a plate of toasted bread and jam. I told her we didn't ask for any food. She said it was a special request from the man at the bar. I looked, and it was the man with the bushy beard and the Hurricane-sad eyes. He did a little wave, and we waved back.

No, said canoe woman number two. He didn't kill anything. At least I don't think so. Should we even be talking about this. I don't think we should talk about this.

The two-second dreamer entered the teahouse by opening the door and jumping in. He yelled, Everything always feels like a dream because it probably is.

Everyone at the bar laughed. The two-second dreamer, smiling, not seeing me, went up to them and took a seat. Black tea, he said.

He was different before, I said. I told a short story about Iamso, when we built the pipeline and how quiet he was with his books.

He's scared of death, of being forgotten, of being washed away and having no one to take care of the future, she said. So he writes everywhere. It makes sense.

But he didn't kill the Hurricane, I repeated.

No, she said. And I think we should stop right there and enjoy our tea. We could talk more about your marriage to Helena. Or we could talk more about the new factory. Have you eaten anything from there yet. It's not too bad.

I wanted to repeat, But he didn't kill the Hurricane, except it was too late, because the two-second dreamer· had come over to our table and said he was having nightmares.

Karen

Someone please help me.

Daniel

After canoe woman number two left, I asked the two-second dreamer about his nightmares. He said they involved the Hurricane, but he was too scared to say anything. When people asked for a two-second dream and he was paid for it, he lied and gave them dreams containing fields of horses.

It's because Iamso didn't do anything to the Hurricane. The Hurricane is still there, somewhere.

I know, he said.

But everyone seems so happy.

Because there's no reason to be sad. But they aren't happy either. They are somewhere between.

How awful.

I asked if I could hear one of his two-second

nightmares, and he said no, it would infect my mood and, if I told anyone, probably drive the town to madness. Things are fine, he said. Let me buy you a cup of cold black tea.

Our windless days expanded. Helena and I looked older, but we acted the same. With more people we almost ran out of food, but the tiny factory produced more. Iamso hurried to write over the new machinery parts.

One day a wave broke in the ocean and people felt the word Hurricane begin to roll from their tongues, but they held back.

The man with the bushy beard and the Hurricane-sad eyes died in his sleep, as everyone else did who reached a certain age. We didn't know the definition of the Hurricane, and we didn't know the definition of disease.

Helena and I stopped trying to have a child. She tried to act like everything was fine, smiling with everyone else, but there were tears in her eyes.

The town grew larger, stretching around half the mountain. My evening walks became less and less lonely.

The mountain was so warm now that the younger people in town stopped wearing clothes. No need for them, they said. The mountain, blanketed in graffiti Iamso, produced a few plumes of smoke every few months.

When I told Helena I believed that Iamso never killed

the Hurricane—who could—she put her finger over my lips and then undressed herself.

It could come back, I said. I sat on the edge of the bed, my head almost touching the ceiling, my shoulders hunched over.

Doesn't matter, she said, getting into bed. We'll climb to the top of the mountain and let it pass. Or we'll bear the heat and hide inside the mountain for a day. Why is it you can't understand we're safe now.

Because we're not.

Helena lay behind me and pulled my shoulders back until I was twisted, turned, and was on top of her. Outside, another blank sky and full sun, people simple and happy, who didn't look at the horizon anymore.

It was morning, and canoe woman number two stood outside our home screaming that the Hurricane was coming back. He was gathering clouds and working his way up from the bottom of the ocean, she said. She spent the previous night filling tea bags with dirt and sand and stacking them around her home. There were thousands of them. She had painted the house neon blue and boarded up the windows.

I covered her mouth with my hand and whispered through my fingers for her to stop. I looked around. No one else was in the streets yet. People had been following Iamso for years, staying up late and getting up to witness only a few hours of the sun.

I took my hand away and felt tears on my fingertips. I wanted to tell her everything would be okay, but Iamso would do that, so I walked back inside my house and held Helena, who was pushed up against the wall and window, still asleep.

The two-second dreamer stopped giving out two-second dreams. He said he didn't dream anymore, but the real reason was the nightmares. He told me this over cold black tea. The water in his eyes trembled, and his skin was ash-colored. He was losing his hair. He whispered every sentence. He had stopped sleeping. When Iamso asked him for a dream, he lied, made something up, said he looked so poorly because he was working so hard. The fake dreams repeated themselves, and Iamso stopped asking for them.

Eventually the two-second dreamer disappeared. Someone said she saw him climb the mountain and throw himself off, but no one found a body. Another said that was wrong, that he climbed the mountain and disappeared into the peak, where the smoke came from.

Iamso held an audition for a new two-second dreamer. Oliver and Peter were there to help. They settled on a young boy with blond hair and sandy brown eyes who had the ability to fall asleep on command and regulate the duration of his sleep.

With some practice he could hand out two-second, five-minute, or one-hour dreams, said Iamso.

I walked around the mountain one evening looking for the two-second dreamer's body. I saw an arm dangling from a ledge on the mountain and climbed up. It was him. His eyes were open, and I closed them with my fingertips. I carried the body down the mountain, over the painted fields of graffiti Iamso. I found a washed-up abandoned pipe, one of the originals, and put the two-second dreamer inside. I pushed his body in one end and pulled his arms from the other side. I rolled him into the calm sea.

Karen

I pull my legs to my chest and lie on my side as the rain gets heavy again. A group of men cheer and scream that we are saved. Help is here.

Daniel

Another day, and Helena finds a glob of hard black rock in the street. It has waves and skin that smokes. Later people talk about something landing in the street, a great big thud, when we're all drunk on tea.

Karen

It's either waves or someone else is trying to get into this raft. I can't move to look. I've taken off my socks and am using them as bandages. I'm going to be saved, and Daniel, too.

The water is calm.

Daniel

The tiny factory became a large factory, and more pipelines were built and fed into the ocean. The man who called himself Scientist found a way to grow crops faster with a new soil. He studied the mountain and its growing warmth and told Iamso it wasn't a mountain but something else. That we should wish for snow.

Karen

I failed Daniel. I'm falling asleep.

Daniel

Who will die first, I asked Helena.

We were waist-high in the ocean. I made waves with my hand so I could remember what they looked like.

Helena dove under the water and reappeared farther away. I thought about writing our life story on a side of the mountain. I thought about Helena disappearing again. She was so far away in the ocean now. I shouted and told her that if she goes any farther, she'll fall off the horizon. She laughed and moments later swam between my legs.

I'm back, she said, and wiped the water from her eyes.

It's always like that, I said.

Oliver died next, in his sleep, during a nap. Stella was a mess. She dug a trench down her forearm with a broken teacup before Iamso and Peter wrapped pig fat around the wound. She slept for twelve days. When she woke, they held an audition for a new Oliver.

That one, she said, pointing to Peter.

Iamso looked at Peter. Peter walked up to Stella and kissed her lips.

I stood next to Helena. Someone ran along the horizon.

A week later Peter died. Choosing Peter had been a horrible mistake for Stella. Iamso wanted her to pick someone younger, who would live much longer. Stella was a trembling mess fixated on the sky. She covered her head and pulled out her matted hair in clumps.

Karen

What we always said to each other: *Everything will be okay*. But we never really tried to fix anything. We just said, *Everything will be okay*.

One night we went out with a bunch of friends for drinks, and Daniel was in a good mood. Past midnight we walked through an empty parking lot scattered with shopping carts. Daniel ran ahead of us with our friend Peter. They ran with the shopping carts until they fell down laughing. Daniel yelled at the night sky when he stood up. He shook a fist, and we laughed, and I thought, *Everything will be okay*, even though I didn't feel it.

Daniel

I saw you, says Helena. With her, outside.

Everyone in town is worried about the mountain. It's producing more clouds, and the strange hot rocks look like molds of small rivers. I've heard waves crashing in the middle of the night, and they are not in my dreams.

With who, I say.

We walk around the mountain. Twelve men paint the sand with graffiti Iamso, where the waves crashed the night before. They hold pieces of paper with Iamso's words in one hand and a paintbrush in the other. They won't admit the ocean is moving once again. They give us dirty looks.

You've picked a new Helena, haven't you.

No, no I haven't.

The other morning, she says. I wasn't going to say anything. But I looked out the window, and you were standing in the street with canoe woman number two. You had your hand over her mouth, and you were holding her. She was upset. You had a big fight.

I don't really know her, I say.

Before he died, says Helena, the two-second dreamer said you were at the teahouse with her. He saw you.

That's true, I say. But you're my wife. I lost you and found you, and I wouldn't do anything to lose you again.

I'm leaving, she says. I'll tell Iamso I want a new husband.

You can't do that. I love you, I say.

And you'll have your new Helena. Things will be okay.

I tried talking to Helena as we rounded the moun- | *201* tain, but she wouldn't listen. I told her about the scraps of paper, the question I had asked the entire town. I told her what canoe woman number two had said. I told her that she tried keeping it a secret but it drove her mad, and that's when she was screaming in the street, and I woke and ran out and tried to quiet her. I told her about the tea bags filled with sand surrounding her house and how sad it was. I thought Helena said something about us not having children, but I could be wrong, because she was running away, leaving me again and again and again.

I can't sleep, I told Iamso.

Could you ever sleep, he said.

What.

Do you want a new Helena. We can arrange it. The only thing I ask is to have my name written on her wrists.

No, I don't want that anymore.

The bed was lonely. I listened to the others in the room snoring and making love. It was so cramped now. I felt like I was sleeping inside a tight section of pipe. The wind picked up again, rattling the windows.

More people died, and more people were born. Iamso grew old, then younger-looking, and then I had the thought that maybe the original Iamso had died and the one I was looking at was a replacement, a new Iamso.

I liked it when we worked on the first pipeline, I told him one day while swimming. I even liked meeting the deserts and that underground village and rescuing the village of underwater pipes.

What, said Iamso.

The first thing you ever drew, that image, what was it.

I can't understand what you're saying.

He kept bobbing up and down in the water, swimming to the bottom, where he was writing on the ocean floor.

No one mentioned the clouds pushed up from the horizon. No one mentioned the waves. No one mentioned the boiling mountain that wasn't a mountain but what the Scientist called a volcano. No one mentioned these things because they were new to us.

How did I survive.

Was I a new version of myself.

Helena disappeared for two days and reappeared

with a new husband who was a much younger and better-looking version of me.

I left the house and tried to sleep outside. It was so hot. I couldn't understand how anyone could sleep. I lay on the ground and stared at the black sky. I looked to the right and saw the horizon crack with lightning, imagined beneath the ocean the churning of mud, the shoving of fish, a death-rattle undertow calling me. I looked to the left and up and saw the mountain dripping hot red liquid from a stone peak once green. I closed my eyes and recalled the first poem Iamso wrote for me, Helena pulling away from me, the floor black as night and scattered with stars.

Iamso couldn't continue the lie anymore that he had killed the Hurricane, because the Hurricane was shutting down the sky.

One morning a mob formed, screaming and shouting for Iamso to admit that he hadn't done anything. That he only gave the town false hope. That he had ripped his own clothes, bitten his own arm for teeth marks, bloodied his mouth with his own knuckles. Things people read and learned from the writing on the mountain.

Everything will be okay, he said. Really, trust me.

Someone yanked his arm, and he fell to the ground, half the mob still yelling, the other half pointing to the sky and the horizon, saying that yes, it was back. Not one person looked at the mountain that oh, so badly wanted to boil over, burn a hundred paths through the town and into the sea.

Tell the truth, Iamso, someone said.

He fell to his knees and vomited blue, yellow, red, purple, all colors, pale and neon, all graffiti, into a massive liquid pool. The mob's circle expanded as the pool filled.

We have nowhere to hide, someone said, looking at the horizon.

Karen

Eyes closed, I feel the raft rock from side to side, hear the soft splashing of water as the rain falls and this city is flooded and looted.

Daniel, I think. *What was it like to be you?*

Daniel

I knew this would happen, said canoe woman number two. There's no way to kill a Hurricane. It's such a silly idea, to want to kill a Hurricane.

What came first was the hot red liquid from the mountain, which the Scientist called lava.

It's called a volcano, he said, and jotted something down in his book.

We really tried our best to believe in Iamso, didn't we, said canoe woman number two.

The town was flailing arms. A desperate attempt to fill tea bags with sand was made. They created a quick village of pipes. Get in, someone yelled. Everyone get in. But these pipes weren't like my pipes. They were small and narrow and could barely fit a baby.

Try to put the babies inside the pipes, someone said. Stuff their mouths with enough bread and jam for a week and send them out to sea. Someone will eventually find them.

The first lava path destroyed an entire section of mountain, an entire book of graffiti Iamso.

Iamso stood bent over at the colored-vomit pool, purple flowing from his mouth.

I was barefoot and wet and burning up with heat. I thought, I want Helena, any Helena, please give me my wife back.

Iamso tried. He built a wall around the base of the volcano from pieces of pipe. He explained that it was a special type of pipe material, and the blacksmiths shrugged their shoulders and said nothing.

When a piling of hot waves and then the mad rush of lava came down the volcano, it seared a perfect path through the pipe wall and into the sea.

One of the workers who'd built my bed threw himself into the path of lava. He said it was all in the mind, the heat. We watched in disbelief as he climbed a section of the pipe wall, jumped, and disappeared.

Sections of the mountain, this thing called volcano, created burning streets that then created ropes of mountain that we lived on, waving to one another across the smoldering fog, the bubbling lava that people prayed to cool.

I sat on my strip of mountain and watched the ocean churn foam. I couldn't remember the last time I slept. I closed my eyes to remember and was soon pulled out to sea, flipping and somersaulting underwater. I swam in one direction and only saw the sea darken, so I swam in the opposite direction and clawed at hot sand. I looked above the water, gasped for air, and saw an entire town of Helenas, all telling me to come back to bed, there is a family here to take care of and place hope in.

When I got back onto land, I was on a different strip of mountain, this one much thinner, fewer people. Canoe woman number two said she needed a new husband, and I said okay, Helena, Karen, whoever you are.

YOU ARE SKELETON. That's what I read on the volcano wall, the graffiti Iamso in midnight blue letters.

Helena asked if I ever slept, and I said I probably will very soon.

The waves crashed and pulled at my toenails.

I told Helena I loved her. The sky was a mix of dust, cloud, and smoldering lava fog. We tried to predict which one of us would die first and how.

The Hurricane, she said. A series of strong winds and

then one huge wave, a new wave. If anyone survives, it will be called the New Year's Wave.

Me too, I said. The volcano is so . . . I don't know the word for it.

New.

That's it. The Hurricane is more of a tradition. Did I ever tell you I lived a short while in a village of underwater pipes. I spent one night running around and looking for you.

No, she said. But that sounds very . . . chivalrous.

That's it, I said. It was. Maybe I'll tell you about it sometime.

I'd like that, she said.

Bridges appeared as thin strands of cooled lava. When you walked over to another strip of land, the lava below was so hot it singed the hairs on your legs. A dress would easily go up in flames. I saw Peter's mouth in the lava below.

It's not as hot over here, said Helena. Maybe you can try to sleep.

I said okay and lay down on the warm rock. When I looked up, over my feet, waves leaped into the air. I put my head back and closed my eyes and tried to remember the first two-second dream I had received.

I didn't think it would end like this, said Helena.

Someone told us to grab a bucket and fill it with ocean water. People poured the water onto the streets of lava, and small puffs of steam rose, but nothing cooled. They prayed for the lava to stop. Homes floated away in the lava, their yellow-colored roofs drifting by, flowing into the ocean, whose waves pushed them back at us.

The pipeline melted and disappeared. Everything that Iamso had worked so hard to cover with his words, his name, evaporated, burned, softened to mud, and was covered by either lava or the ocean.

I want to have dreams, I told Helena. Like the ones the two-second dreamer had. Did you know that his final dreams were of this. He didn't want to tell anyone. They weren't dreams, but nightmares.

Helena was about to answer when her head snapped to the side like a stick and her eyes forgot how to blink.

A wave had rushed over us, carrying us past the lava, my hand burned to the bone, blood in thin strings stretched out in the ocean, my body then bouncing off the volcano, scraping skin over the dirt and sand, then into the depths of the ocean, and I tried to open my eyes to see a Helena, anyone.

This time there wasn't any village of underwater pipes or a new mountain. The factory sank to the bottom of the ocean as I swam to the top, where there was a light, where I thought the sky would be.

I swam toward a shadow above, swam around it and into the air. It was a rowboat. I tipped it to the side and climbed in, hoping to see Helena in it, but it was a different woman, crumpled at one end.

I pulled her legs out and put my ear against her mouth, but she wasn't breathing.

In the distance, waves swallowed the volcano, bursts of lava exploded into the air, seeping into the ocean, warming the water that splashed into the rowboat.

We rode over waves, my hands gripping each side,

and I shifted my weight from side to side, looking at the dead woman at the end of the rowboat.

I was sure there was a new sky behind this sky and new mountains to be found through the smoke and mist, and a new ocean beneath these waves, but I didn't see any of them. I didn't see anything but myself, here, sitting in a rowboat with a pale woman void of breath, hoping for the Hurricane to die down again.

I curled myself into the other end of the rowboat and wished to fall asleep before anything more could be possible. Maybe if I peeked over the edge of this boat, I'd see a mountain, a volcano, an island to start over.

A boat horn blew across the sky. It got closer and closer. A machine with a propeller flew above and dropped a ladder. My eyes felt heavy, and I thought, That's my wife in the rowboat with me. I could recognize her now. She was the woman who came from the woods, the woman who called my name. I'm Daniel. I'm Daniel. I'm Daniel, and my wife is here with me.

End

Acknowledgments

Very special thanks to the following people: Tom Roberge, Allison Lorentzen, Taylor Sperry, Stephen Morrison, Kathryn Court, Bill Clegg, Shaun Dolan, Sonya Cheuse, Blake Butler, Adam Robinson, Kristen Iskandrian, Lily Hoang, Chris LaBarge, John and Joy, Blake, Nicole, and Mom and Dad.

AVAILABLE FROM PENGUIN

Light Boxes
A Novel

ISBN 978-0-14-311778-0

The inhabitants of one closely knit town are experiencing perpetual winter. A godlike spirit who lives in the sky, named February, is punishing the town for flying and has banned flight of all kind, including hot air balloons and children's kites. It's February who makes the sun nothing but a faint memory, who blankets the ground with snow, who freezes the rivers and the lakes. As endless winter continues, children go missing and a growing number of adults become nearly catatonic with depression—but others find the strength to fight back.

PENGUIN
BOOKS